# BLAME IT ON

## *the kiss*

### A KISSES IN THE SAND STORY

# ROBIN BIELMAN

Previously released on Entangled's Bliss imprint.

Entangled Publishing, LLC
2614 South Timberline Road
Suite 109
Fort Collins, CO 80525
Visit our website at www.entangledpublishing.com.

Lovestruck is an imprint of Entangled Publishing, LLC.

Edited by Wendy Chen
Cover design by Heather Howland
Cover art from iStock

Manufactured in the United States of America

First Edition June 2015

*For Samanthe Beck, who always knows the right thing to say. Your brilliance helped make this book what it is. Thank you from the bottom of my heart.*

# Chapter One

A girl knew her love life had hit a low point when adolescent kissing games got her hot and bothered.

Honor Mitchell leaned against the wall in the dark hallway closet and wondered which lucky guy would pick her location, and if his mouth-to-mouth skills would satisfy this sudden jolt of eagerness. This wasn't exactly the way she'd envisioned breaking her dry spell, but since her entire focus the past few months had been on fulfilling her best friend's wish and opening their new store; she hadn't had much time for anything else.

She took a deep breath and ran her tongue over her bottom lip. A little innocent fun was just what the Stress Fairy ordered. The last time she'd wanted to kiss a guy... she blinked away *that* memory and thanked her lucky stars he hadn't arrived at Zane and Sophie's combined bachelor/ bachelorette party yet.

She'd been mentally preparing herself to see him for the past week, but needed a little more time. Another thirty years would be good, but she probably had more like thirty minutes.

*Come on already.* Where was her "One Minute Temptation" stud? With an equal number of single guys and girls someone had to show up to her spot. She thrummed her fingers against the sides of her jean-clad thighs. Under no circumstance would she leave the closet. Not until she fulfilled her end of the game. As one of three bridesmaids, she had an obligation to follow through on all tasks, requests, and activities.

Sophie's future sister-in-law had planned the games for tonight, and Honor found it cute that she'd included ones Sophie hadn't played as a teenager. Of course Sophie and Zane had slid into the same dark room and who knew when they'd pop back out, but that only made this party game that much better for her dear friend. Sophie had the guy of her dreams and in three days she'd be his wife.

Honor closed her eyes. *Wife.* Something she'd never be. She'd been super excited when Sophie asked her to be a bridesmaid, though, forgetting that meant being in close proximity to Zane's best friends and groomsmen for the long weekend celebration.

One hurt-to-look-at groomsman in particular.

A few weeks ago, during a girls' night in, Honor had confessed to Sophie how she knew Bryce. Lord, her cheeks still heated just thinking about that night eight months ago. Payton, Honor's best friend since kindergarten, had passed away two months earlier and Honor had needed a distraction. She still missed Payton so much, and not a day went by that Honor didn't say a little something to her BFF.

"I'm standing in a closet, Pay, waiting for a kiss and wishing so hard you were still here."

She had a feeling she'd be celebrating Pay's bachelorette party right about now if Payton hadn't suffered from a rare lung disease that took her friend with little warning. Instead, her best friend had given Honor a list. Not a bucket list, but a

*Things to Do Before I Turn 25* list. And just before she died, she asked Honor for one thing: make her wishes happen.

Honor had never followed through with anything in her own life. Ever. But the request was Payton's last wish and Honor had promised her. Twice, since Payton had made her repeat her oath. The first thing on Pay's list? A one night stand.

Enter Bryce Bishop.

One of Zane's best men and the most delicious specimen of a man she'd ever laid eyes on. And Honor had laid eyes on lots of guys. But being the fun, flirty girl with a short attention span, she never let a guy stick around for very long. Her friends called her a serial dater. Not the Fruity Pebbles kind.

Bryce also happened to be Payton's secret boyfriend.

Payton had been crazy about him, tossing out the L word after only two weeks. Because of the gossip mill in their small town and Pay's previous crappy track record with guys, she'd kept Bryce to herself, the two of them spending all their time together in a bubble of happiness at his place about an hour away. A few days before Honor was supposed to meet the love of her best friend's life, Payton got her diagnosis. Pay broke up with Bryce and ended all communication.

Closing her eyes again, Honor thought back to her first ever one nightstand and how she'd thankfully figured out who he was before—

The closet door opened and shut so fast she didn't have time to catch a glimpse of her gentleman caller. All the guys were nice, though, so she could handle a minute of closed mouth kissing with any of them.

He didn't say anything, but he smelled amazing. A little spicy, a little minty, and… her pulse sped up… a lot familiar. She'd thought about his scent more times than she cared to admit since that night at her dad's law firm's party.

"Bryce?" she whispered, grabbing a coat and pulling it in front of her, like *that* would somehow turn off her senses. Why hadn't she chosen a bathroom or bedroom to wait in instead of a closet with little room to move? Or make an escape?

"Honor?" His deep, amiable voice sounded just as surprised.

"When did you get here?"

"Just now. Sophie greeted me and pushed me in here. What's going on?"

That sneaky little bride-to-be. Honor never should've confessed her situation with Bryce. But after drinking one too many coffees with help from Baileys, her lips had let loose. She hated herself for having even the slightest inappropriate thought about Bryce. He'd been Payton's. Should still be. And she'd made out with him! Honor couldn't look at him without thinking about her best friend and how happy and in love she'd been with him.

"We're in the middle of a game." Honor let go of the jacket and tried to relax. Were the walls closing in? She fanned her sweater away from her stomach.

"A game?"

Honor's eyes adjusted to the darkness and she could just make out Bryce's broad shoulders and the outline of his head. She didn't need any light to picture his soft, tidy brown hair, dark cinnamon eyes, and the cleft in his chin that made her insides go all lovey-dovey. "Yes, you know, an activity or contest often played during a party?" Self defense and shame dictated the flippant remark rather than a simple yes.

"Hmm…"

Before he could follow up that far too appealing sound, she continued. "And since you missed out on the rules and stuff, we can just head back to the party."

"Tell me the rules, Honor." His tone rang curious. And far too rebellious for her liking.

She gulped. Ran her sweaty palms down her jeans. "I'd really rather skip it."

"Because of me?" He inched a little closer, his body heat and knock-a-girl-to-her-knees scent completely surrounding her now.

"Bryce." How could he not feel as guilty as she did about what had happened between them?

"I want to know. We're part of a wedding for the next three days and I don't want things to be awkward. You avoided me like I had some deadly disease during the film festival a few months ago, but you can't keep dodging me now. If this is about what happened—"

"Stop."

His hand found hers. He laced their fingers together and so much pleasure shot up her arm she had to hold back a sigh. "You don't need to be—"

"I said stop. Please." Humiliation filled her chest and the back of her throat all over again. She couldn't get past the moment when they'd finally exchanged names and she'd fled his hotel room with her dress haphazardly covering her body.

She tried to pull her hand away, but he wouldn't let go. "We need to clear the air. Walk through that night and..." he let out a deep breath, "move past it. I've tried to leave it behind, but I'm having a hard time forgetting how good it felt to touch you. If we hadn't exchanged names..."

Her breath caught somewhere between her lungs and her vocal chords, so it took her a minute to answer. He was right about them talking. She didn't want to feel weird about things during the wedding festivities. She didn't want to cause Sophie any concern or strain during this special time. If they discussed that night like two mature adults, she could walk out of this closet with their very brief past over and done with.

"You were supposed to be a one night stand."

He let go of her hand and shifted his stance. "Yeah? When did you decide that?" He sounded half relieved, half sheepish. Had he been after the same thing? Had he wanted to use her to forget about Payton?

"After you laughed at my lawyer joke. No, wait, after you told me you hated stuffy, everyone has stick-up-their-asses parties and you'd rather swim with sharks."

"Then *you* laughed," he said. "And it was the best sound I'd ever heard. I whispered I'd get a room at the hotel and asked you to sneak away with me."

Bryce liked her laugh? She sounded like a hyena on helium. They'd never talked about what they were both doing at the party, just formed an immediate kinship over feeling like they'd rather be any place else.

"And I said yes, because that's when I decided what I wanted to do." Everything about Bryce had made her insides dance and sing. He'd lit her up so much more than she'd ever been before. After only an hour together! That's when she knew she'd had to take the *Pretty Woman* approach. No kissing on the mouth. Lame movie move she'd never used before, but following Julia Roberts' lead had seemed like a good idea at the time.

"For the record, you would've been my first one night stand."

"Really?" she almost said. A hot guy like him never having a quick hook-up seemed improbable, but in case he wasn't feeding her a line she went with, "That's nice to know."

"Why do I get the feeling there's more to your story?"

His suspicion sent a wave of warmth through her. He'd been in tune with her that night, but she wanted him nowhere near her feelings now. She swallowed. How much should she tell him?

"My emotions were all over the place that night. And then I met you and I forgot for a little while, and…"

"What?"

"Then I remembered Payton's list and that's why I went to a room with you."

"Her list?"

"Before she died she gave me a list of things she'd always wanted to accomplish and asked me to do them for her. I agreed without even looking at it. She'd been my very best friend for almost twenty years, and there was nothing I wouldn't do for her." Honor's heart gave that familiar hitch whenever she thought about Payton and how unfair it was that her life had been cut so short.

"A one night stand was on her list?"

"Yes."

Silence filled the small space. Not the good kind. Or the comfortable kind. The kind that screamed she'd said too much. She couldn't believe she'd told him. But if they were going to move past what happened between them, she had to be honest.

"Until that night I had no idea Payton had passed away. When you told me it was like being thrown against a wall of razor blades. She'd dumped me, by voicemail, with no explanation, and ignored my calls and texts…"

"She didn't want to burden you."

"No. She didn't trust me to be there for her."

The darkness, combined with the hurt in Bryce's voice pressed down on Honor, making their cramped area feel ten times smaller.

"I'm sorry." Truthfully, Honor had no idea how Payton really felt. Her friend had refused to talk about Bryce after the break-up.

"You have no reason to be."

"Don't I?"

Several seconds passed before he said, "If we'd kept things anonymous, would you have gone through with it?"

She wanted to believe she would have. "I'm not sure. I'm not really wired for sex with a stranger." She flirted and had fun with guys all the time, but it rarely went beyond a hand on the arm or peck on the cheek. She'd dated plenty of guys over the years, sure, most of them jerks, a few of them decent, none of them like Bryce.

"Correct me if I'm wrong, but by the time we went to my room I didn't feel like we were strangers. I don't confide to just any girl that I wore pull-ups until I was five."

"That's right." She couldn't help herself and let out a small giggle-sigh kind of sound, glad he'd broken some of the tension. They had gotten to know each other like it was the most natural thing in the world. Which made her wonder again… "What about you? You didn't know what had happened to Payton, and claim you'd never had a one night stand before. Was I just a rebound?"

He didn't say anything, but she felt his eyes bore into hers.

"That's one way of putting it," he finally confessed.

"What's the other way?" His admission stung. It was bad enough they'd had their hands all over each other, but to find out he'd used her to get over Payton made her feel dirty as well as guilty.

"So what else is on Payton's list?" he asked instead of answering her.

The question, along with his unresponsiveness, raised the hairs on the back of her neck. "None of your business."

His posture changed, the air between them rippling with uncomfortable waves. "Should've guessed that. What's on yours?"

"I don't have a list." How could she when she never saw anything through to the end? She didn't need any more pressure than Payton's five wishes. A tiny part of her was pretty damn angry with her best friend for thrusting such a responsibility on her. Payton knew she didn't focus on anything for very long. A free spirit, everyone said.

Yeah, their whole small Southern California town of White Strand Cove knew all about Honor's lack of commitment.

Her high school boyfriend had made sure of it.

"We should head back to the party now." She pushed off from the wall and bumped right into his chest. When had he inched closer?

"Can't." His warm, peppermint breath fanned her face.

She took a step back—one measly step and her butt hit the wall. "When can you?"

"Are we good?"

"Yes, we're good." Sort of. She did feel better for having talked things out. She'd just ignore the way a simple look at him made her think things she absolutely should not. Could not.

"Then we're halfway there." He lifted his arms and flattened his hands on the wall on either side of her head, trapping her.

Her heart did a three-sixty. Slippery didn't begin to describe her palms. And he smelled so yummy that she wiggled her nose to stop from breathing him in. "What are you doing and what does halfway mean?"

"It means as soon as you tell me about the game we're supposed to play, we can leave the closet." His tone had taken an edge she hadn't heard from him before. Part bad boy, part bitter, like he'd detached himself from their past and their history with Payton.

"I think game time's over."

"I think the only game that comes to my mind that's played in a closet with a beautiful girl has got to do with kissing. *Seven Minutes in Heaven* or something like that. And since we are in the wedding party, it's our duty to follow through, right?"

He thought she was beautiful?

Tingles swept over her lips and down the backs of her arms.

"Am I right?"

She cleared her throat and told her body to ignore any more tingles, quivers, flutters, shivers, trembles, prickles, or shudders he might instigate. He belonged to her best friend, even if she wasn't here to claim him. "Yes, it's a kissing game. But *the rules* say one minute."

"So you planned to kiss the guy that found you in here?"

"Yes."

"On the mouth?" he asked, surprised.

"Yes. But no tongue."

The small space between them dissolved as he canted his head down to talk in her ear. "I think it's our obligation to play, Honor. It's just a game, so can I kiss you?"

*YES!* Her traitorous body shouted as his husky voice made her toes curl. Then, like he had some magic mojo, she put her arms around his neck. Her hands should not have been anywhere but at her sides, dammit. She reasoned the dark had something to do with it. Because she couldn't really see him, she could pretend he was Theo James and this was her sixty seconds of pretend boyfriend kissing.

"We shouldn't."

"I know."

Maybe it was his agreement. Maybe it was her earlier desire to break her dry spell, to not leave the closet until she'd gotten a kiss. Whatever it was, she found herself pushing aside her guilt and wanting to finish the game she'd agreed to play.

"Okay," she said.

"You sure?"

God, did he have to be so careful with her? She touched her nose to his. "Yes."

"Plan on one minute in heaven, Honor." A split second later his lips were on hers.

Her eyes fluttered shut and the only man she pictured as his mouth moved against hers with a feather-light touch was Bryce Bishop. His sexy smile and gorgeous, milk chocolate latte eyes had been burned into the back of her eyelids since the second they'd met.

And as she feared, their mouths were a seamless, perfect fit. He kissed her with super soft, slow, confident brushes of his sensuous lips, his jaw relaxed. No guy had ever started a kiss like this. With thoughtful determination and just the right amount of pressure. All those uptight cells of hers went languid. Her fingers played with the soft hair at the back of his neck.

He cupped her cheeks in his warm hands, and his tender onslaught felt so good she never wanted it to end. His lips were like sugar and honey, and tasted a million times better than she'd imagined over the past several months. He moved his mouth against hers with confidence. Skill.

She almost took his hands and moved them to her hips so she could press her body against his. Kissing him put her hormones into overdrive and she needed more. Much more. This gentle, closed mouth technique of his had it going on, and she craved an openmouthed kiss more than she did her next breath.

A tiny purr escaped her lips. She couldn't help it. The corners of his mouth lifted in return and he eased off just a bit. She grabbed him by the back of the shirt to make sure he stayed put.

That night in his hotel room, his kisses to her neck and shoulder, the inside of her palm and wrist, had been incredible and dreamy, but this kiss?

With each soft caress he seemed to take as much pleasure from it as she did, and knowing she affected him put this unplanned lip lock into a stratosphere all by itself.

She slipped the tip of her tongue over his bottom lip, ready to move to the next level, but he pulled back. The sudden loss was like having a cold bucket of water dumped over her head.

"What's wrong?" she whispered.

"Nothing. Just sticking to the rules."

Thank goodness one of them had a conscience at the moment. His lips had turned her into an unthinking body where her edges softened and her insides melted.

"Friends?" he asked.

"Friends," she half lied. She'd do whatever necessary for the wedding, but nothing more. The horror at what she'd just done set in. She'd been able to forgive herself for her past indiscretion because she hadn't known who Bryce was. But tonight she'd knowingly kissed him. She blinked back the regretful tears threatening to expose her. He belonged to Payton, and always would. He'd been the last good thing in her best friend's life, and Honor wouldn't sully or poach on that.

Three more days. That's all she had to get through and then she'd be free and clear of Bryce Bishop.

• • •

Bryce slipped two fingers under his shirt collar, pulled the material away from his neck, and took a step back before he changed his mind and committed an all-out assault on Honor's incredible mouth. He wished she hadn't tasted so good.

All those months ago when they'd first met, he'd thought her the perfect girl to help him shed his good guy image. Being the committed, serious relationship type had gotten him nothing but heartache, and he'd wanted a night of no strings attached fun. She'd seemed up for that, too.

Until Payton had come between them.

Payton. Just thinking her name hurt like hell. He'd loved her and she'd trampled all over his heart. Messing around with Honor had almost ruined what little self preservation he'd had left. What a brutal twist of fate that the first girl to spark his interest since Payton was her best friend. Talk about a slap in the face. Guilt had plagued him because he felt like he'd disrespected Payton, and he hated feeling like a bad guy when she had done *him* wrong.

Having the chance to talk with Honor after she'd dogged him at the film festival a few months back brought him a better sense of closure, but he couldn't deny he was still attracted to her. Or that knowing she'd set out to do something for her best friend when it wasn't her style intrigued him.

Which meant he needed his head examined. He'd made new rules: Never get too attached and never give a woman the power to damage his heart again. One look at Honor made those rules hard to remember. Until mention of Payton jogged his memory. Honor reminded him of what he'd lost, and no doubt supported Payton's decision to cut all ties with him. He couldn't trust her. Not by a long shot.

Whatever simmered between them ended in this closet. The kiss just now had been selfish, a lingering desire left over from their night at the hotel.

"Come on. We've got a party to get back to." He opened the closet door and blinked a few times to adjust to the bright light. Voices echoed down the hall from the kitchen and living room area.

Honor slipped by him. "Thank you."

He grabbed her hand. She spun around and ended up flush against him with her palm pressed to his chest. Her blue-gray eyes sparkled under long, dark lashes, and for a moment he forgot what he was going to say. "What are you doing after the party?" he asked, to get a rise out of her. She brought out a little devil in him.

"I, um—"

"There you are," Sophie said, walking up behind Honor. "Everything okay?"

Honor wheeled back around. "Absolutely. What's up?"

"You're my toilet paper bride." Sophie turned. "Come on."

Bryce followed Honor, who followed Sophie. His eyes roamed over Honor's backside, from her small back covered in a form fitting lilac sweater, to her waist, to the curve of her hips and her shapely rear end in a pair of tight jeans.

She looked over her shoulder. "I'm busy," she mouthed.

It took him a second to understand she meant later. He nodded, knowing full well she'd answer his question that way.

They reached the large living room with floor to ceiling windows that allowed for views of the ocean, and he headed for his best friend, Zane. "Dude," Bryce said, patting him on the back and shaking his hand. "It's not too late to back out."

Sophie punched him in the biceps right before Zane put his arm around her and brought his bride-to-be close. "Shh," Zane said. "Don't give her any ideas."

Zane and Sophie eyed each other with love and admiration, confirming for the thousandth time that they belonged together. "It's good to see you so happy, man."

"How'd your trip go?" Zane asked.

"He signed, so great." As a sports agent, Bryce had a small list of athletes he represented. Zane garnered him the most return as one of the best pro surfers in the world, but being friends since childhood mattered more than their business partnership. Bryce had spent the past couple of weeks in Seattle with the man he was most proud to add to his agented family: A guy whose body hadn't been whole since he sat behind the wheel of a Humvee in Iraq three years ago. Today he beat practically everyone in Tough Mudders and Spartan competitions, and sat poised to prove even down a leg, physical fitness was about dedication and perseverance.

After the year Bryce had had, things were finally starting to look up.

"Congratulations." Zane gave him a knuckle tap.

"Let's hope my luck holds and I sign the local boy I've got my sights on next."

"Okay everyone," Zane's sister, Julia, said, drawing Bryce's attention to the middle of the room. "It's time for one more game before we eat."

Julia started an explanation, but Bryce lost track the second he glanced across the room and caught Honor looking at him. Their gazes collided. She looked away, but he didn't. Two seconds later, her eyes were back on his.

This time she kept staring. With her long dark blond hair pulled up into a messy bun on top of her head, and full, watermelon red lips, she made his breathing come out a little too fast. She pulled in her bottom lip with her teeth, and he tried not to remember how sweet her mouth tasted.

He couldn't believe how much that chaste kiss had rocked his world. It had taken all his willpower to pull back when he'd felt the tip of her tongue. His thoughts raced to Payton. Had their first kiss been as potent? He gave himself a mental slap. Comparing his first reaction to the two best friends was a stupid thing to do, but being with Honor brought back memories. Memories best left forgotten because all they did was keep him stuck in a place he didn't like.

Someone tugged Honor's arm, stealing her attention.

Bryce heard the words "toilet paper" and "bride," and Julia handed him his very own roll as the party guests got into two groups. Sophie's cousin stood poised to be the bride in his group. Honor had been chosen in the other group.

He knew because as hard as he tried, he couldn't pull his eyes away from her. His other best friend Danny and a couple of Zane's surf buddies couldn't either. And their hands were all over her. Using the toilet paper as an excuse to touch her shoulders, waist, the back of her neck. Honor laughed at something one of the guys said and Bryce's stomach knotted.

"Thanks for the help, bud." Zane bumped his elbow.

Bryce looked down at the full roll of TP still in his hands. Glancing back up, he found Sophie's cousin wore toilet paper from her chest to her knees.

Zane's gaze flicked to Honor and back. "Dude, what are you doing?"

"What?"

"Don't 'what' bullshit me. You were checking out Honor. I thought that ship had sailed." Why he'd told Zane and Danny about his botched one night stand, he didn't know. But when he'd learned that Payton had passed away, they'd plied him with beers to make him feel better and he'd talked.

"It has."

"Might want to tone down the possessive glare then." Zane put a hand on his shoulder. "Besides, I doubt Danny copped a feel. Honor would've kneed him in the balls if he did."

"You've gotten to know her pretty well." Bryce squeezed the Charmin, a double dose of curiosity suddenly coursing through his veins. "What's her deal?"

"She's been a great friend to Sophie. And she's opening up a new shop on Main Street. Something to do with Payton, actually."

Bryce's chest constricted, for Honor this time. He'd heard the pain in her voice earlier, and knew he'd be wrecked if something happened to either Zane or Danny. He also remembered Payton mentioning a dream she and Honor shared. They'd wanted to go into business together.

"Does it have to do with Payton's list?" he wondered aloud, trying to make sense of that new piece of information.

"I've no idea what you're talking about."

"Nothing." Bryce shook his head. Had Honor confided in him something she hadn't shared with Sophie or anyone else?

Unconsciously, his gaze moved to her again. Her arms were spread wide and she twirled, giving her group a good look at their work. A smile lit up her face, playfulness sparkled in her eyes. She was so different from Payton. In looks, in temperament.

He wondered when Payton had written her list. Had it been after she'd dumped him or before? Finding out she wanted a one night stand reopened the crater-sized hole she'd drilled through his heart. He rubbed his chest and turned his back to Honor.

For the next three days he'd do the best man thing and keep Honor at an emotional distance. He'd offered to be friends, but knew that was impossible given her connection to Payton and the wounds not quite healed inside him. Problem was, he'd had his hands and mouth on his ex girlfriend's best friend and forgetting those images was proving difficult. Which put some very unfriendly—and unwelcome—thoughts in his head.

Being attracted to Honor when a part of him couldn't bear to be around her was a burden he wished he didn't have to deal with. She was nothing but trouble to his closed-off heart, and he'd be damned if he forgot that.

*Payton flattened you, dude. Don't think for one second her best friend isn't capable of doing the exact same thing.*

# Chapter Two

"Looks like you're stuck with me," Bryce said in Honor's ear. Despite their best efforts to keep some distance, once again fate had other ideas.

She twisted and narrowed her eyes. "Lucky me." Her sardonic tone brought an involuntary grin to his face.

"You took the words right out my mouth," he fired back, and her gaze dropped to his lips before flying somewhere over his shoulder.

They stood with everyone else in the kitchen, pairing off for the last game of the night. The guys had each picked a partner's name out of a hat and he'd chosen hers.

Julia handed a sheet of paper and canvas bag to each couple. "This is a sexy treasure hunt. You'll see what I mean by reading your list. Some of the hunt items are named, but I've upped the challenge for a few and put clues instead. The team that finds the most items wins. You've got thirty minutes. Go!"

Honor looked over his shoulder at the typed list. "Start in the middle?" she asked, thinking everyone else would start at either the top or bottom.

"My thought exactly." She tugged him away from the others, down a narrow hallway toward the maid's quarters, before snagging the paper out of his hands. "Made in haste, you'll love the taste," she said.

"Sounds like we should've stayed in the kitchen," Bryce said.

"Nope. I'm thinking 'made' as in 'maid' the person, so that's this way." She pushed open the bedroom door and hit the light switch. "See?"

"What am I supposed to see?" Looked like an ordinary room to him.

She rolled her eyes. "The bed." She hurried over to it and put a hand on the rumpled comforter.

Thoughts of the two of them so close to tearing up the sheets the night they'd met immediately ran through his mind. *Shit.* These unwanted memories had to be because he hadn't been with anyone since her, choosing to fly under the radar while his head and heart continued to recuperate.

Honor flung the bedspread aside and there sat one of those large Hershey kisses in a red box for Valentine's Day — the holiday next week. "Get it now?" She lifted the chocolate and tossed it to him.

Smart girl. "Nice job. Where to next?"

She scanned the paper. "Follow me."

He took up the rear without hardship, once again appreciating his view. She led him all around the house. They picked up a pair of fuzzy powder blue handcuffs, a black satin blindfold, and glow in the dark dice with some of his favorite words on them. Laughter and dirty remarks were shared as they crossed paths with others in a race against the clock.

The one item everyone found? Candy condoms. Julia must have bought a hundred-piece bag.

All this sexy treasure hunting had him noticing everything

about his partner. The way she scrunched up her pert nose in concentration when she studied a clue. How her eyes flashed with deep fondness for Sophie whenever they passed one another. But best of all was how her entire face lit up when they found something before another team did.

She was a competitor. Like his clients. Like him.

"I'm thinking this means out front on the grass." She pointed to the last clue on their sheet, her arm grazing his. "What do you think?"

"Blades are green, violets are blue, I want to roll around here, naked with you." Bryce shrugged. "That's probably the worst rhyme I've ever read, but you haven't been wrong yet."

"I know. Right?" She killed him with a smile and hurried out of the house.

Stars littered the moonless sky. Waves crashing in the distance whispered in his ears, and the smell of the ocean and wet sand filled his nose. The tall iron streetlamp at the curb didn't cast much light on the small front yard, so at a quick glance nothing on the grassy area caught his attention.

"I don't see anything," Honor said. "Do you?" She sounded ready to give up and head back in.

"Not yet, but keep looking." He moved his focus from her long legs to the lawn.

"What's that noi—" With only the click of a timer to warn them, the sprinklers popped up and started spraying. Honor spun to frown at him like she had the worst luck in the world and this sort of thing happened all the time.

"Looks like our search just got a little harder," he said.

She shivered, wrapped her arms around herself, and studied him. He could see the wheels turning in her head. Run back into the house or stay and find the last thing they needed?

If there was a way to keep her dry, he would. The temperatures for February had been mild, but it couldn't be more than sixty degrees outside.

"Looks like." She narrowed her eyes, turned, and that's when a stream of water nailed her right in the face. Her hands flew up, she sputtered, her shoulders shook.

Bryce rushed forward to cover her with his body and forget their search, but he stalled when he heard one of the sweetest sounds ever to reach his ears.

Honor's body didn't shake with chills or misery, but with laughter. She cracked up, and apparently couldn't stop. He found himself laughing right along with her until their clothes stuck to their bodies, and she took a deep breath to quiet down.

Water droplets streamed down her face and clung to her eyelashes. She blinked up at him with mischief in her eyes, and the urge to kiss her overwhelmed him. Not like he had in the closet, with care and discretion, but with hunger and passion and pent up desire. He wanted to take her bottom lip between his teeth and deal with the consequences later.

She put two fingers to her mouth to wipe away the moisture. Her chest rose and fell, the wet sweater doing very nice things to her curves. "We, uh, we'd better hurry," she said before twisting around to continue their search.

"Right. Time's almost up." They ducked and weaved through the sprays of water, seeking to end the hunt with one more token in their bag.

"I got it," she shouted from a crouched position. She stood and put something on her finger just as the sprinklers stopped. Her hand lit up. "It's a light up diamond ring." She walked toward him with her arm outstretched so he could check out the toy bling.

He stared at her. Most girls would've had a fit if the sprinklers had soaked them. Not only had Honor laughed it off, she looked amazing and none the worse for wear as the pink light of the ring glowed at her waist.

"Do not tell me you have x-ray vision and can see the color of my undergarments, because then I'd have to use this magic ring to one, make you color blind, and two, make your clothes disintegrate so everyone could see if you're a boxer or briefs man."

His grin came quick and easy. "You want to see what I have on underneath my jeans, all you have to do is ask."

"No thanks." She stopped in front of him.

"You sure?"

"Positive."

"You don't look positive."

"How do I look?"

He took a slow inspection down her body and back up. "You really want me to answer that?"

"Boy, you had me fooled there for a minute Captain Underpants, but I see you're just like every other guy, which is a huge relief, I can't even tell you." She brushed by him and headed toward the front door.

"What does that mean?" He fell in step beside her. Something didn't feel right inside him. He didn't like being lumped in with all guys.

"Here," she slipped the toy ring off her finger and dropped it into their bag. "Be a good partner and turn our stuff in so I can raid Sophie's closest for something to change in to."

"Grab me one of Zane's shirts, would you?"

She paused at the porch to slip off her shoes and slowly rake her eyes down and up his body. *Touché.* "Really? Zane's got all sorts of muscle going on and I'm not sure—"

He whipped off his shirt. Honor was messing with him, but he wanted to remind her Zane didn't have anything on him. He took care of his body, often working out with the guys he represented. He put forth the best image possible for his agency and that included being in good physical shape.

The appreciative look in her eyes told him she liked

what she saw. She'd had her hands all over his chest in their hotel room, and if he closed his eyes he knew he'd remember exactly how hot her touch had made him.

"Can I ask you something?" he ventured.

"Okay," she said to his chest.

"Eyes up here, sweetheart." He motioned his hand in the direction of his face.

Her cheeks reddened. "Sorry, yes?"

"Have you had your one night stand?" He fisted his hands. It didn't matter. It shouldn't matter. But for some reason, he wanted to know. She might not be wired for it, but according to Payton, the two of them were like sisters, and if Honor promised to do the things on Payton's list, he imagined she would keep that vow.

Like the promise she'd probably made to keep him in the dark rather than track him down so he could have been there for Payton, too.

She gulped and again he could see her mind at work in the way she blinked and her head tilted a fraction to the side. "No." A crease drew her brows together. "But I might be able to remedy that these next few days. A couple of Zane's friends seem like they'd be willing to help me out."

No doubt. "People hook up at weddings all the time, don't they?"

"That's what I hear."

"Let me know if I can be of any help."

She raised her eyebrows. "You don't think I can manage this on my own?" Annoyance came through loud and clear, but something else lingered in the depths of her turbulent ocean eyes.

"No. I don't think that at all. I—"

The front door flew open. "Hey," Sophie said. "Here. You guys must be freezing." She handed him a long sleeved thermal shirt and sweatpants, and Honor something pink and gray. "Leave your wet clothes out here, and then come back in for a warm drink. Oh, and I'll take this since time's up." She pulled the canvas bag from his hand and shut the door.

He smiled at the surprise interruption and started to undo the button and zipper on his pants.

Honor's eyes widened and she spun around.

"I'm good with you looking," he said.

"I'm not. Now turn around so I can change, too."

"Funny. You don't strike me as someone modest." He turned and wrangled his wet pants down his legs. Getting the dry sweats and shirt on felt great.

"Oh my god."

He didn't turn or say anything even though the frustration in Honor's voice made it difficult.

"My pants are stuck. I don't think I can get them off without some help. Jesus, wet jeans are heavy and uncooperative."

A grin stretched across his face. "You want my help?"

She let out a deep breath. "Yes, but you have to close your eyes."

"You going commando tonight?" he teased.

"No, but…"

He shut his eyes and turned. She took his outstretched hand and tugged him down to the ground. Once there, she helped him latch on to the bunched up denim at her thighs, he guessed. *Do not peek, Bishop. Do not peek.*

"But?"

"My panties are white and now see-through and there's not a lot to them."

"Gotcha." There wasn't a red-blooded man alive who wouldn't peek. "Let's get these off you." He pulled, she pushed and wiggled, and he got the pants to her feet in no time.

"Thank you," she said, a little out of breath.

"No problem."

"Bryce!"

"What?" Christ, she had sexy legs, and the barely-there material at their juncture left little to the imagination, so his thoughts leaped to about a dozen dirty scenarios.

"Your eyes are open!"

"Yeah, sorry." He jumped to his feet and gave her his back while she mumbled things like jackass and jerkwad as she got dressed.

"I'm done," she huffed.

She wore a pair of loose sweats and had freed her damp hair so it fell past her shoulders. A small black smudge stained the smooth skin underneath her left eye.

He licked his thumb and ran it over the blemish. Her breath caught. "You had something there."

"Honor?" came a guy's voice from the driveway.

Her attention jumped over his shoulder. "Cooper. What are you doing here?"

Bryce turned, and much to his surprise recognized Cooper right away. He'd had a few conversations with him over the phone and they'd met briefly during White Strand's film festival.

"Sophie wanted me to come by." Coop smiled warmly at Honor before turning an eye to him. "Hey dude, I know you, right?"

"Hey, Cooper. Bryce Bishop." He put his hand out.

"Mr. Bishop, that's right." Cooper gave a firm shake. "We've got a meeting next week."

"Hold on," Honor said, stepping between them. "What meeting? How do you guys know each other?"

"I'm hoping to represent him. How do you two know each other?"

Honor put her hands on her hips. "Cooper's my brother."

"Younger brother," Cooper said, "so I'm apologizing now for her over-protectiveness."

Cooper Mitchell was Honor's brother? Shit. He'd never

thought to ask Honor her last name, not that he would have put the two together until now anyway. Coop Mitchell was the local boy Bryce wanted to sign. The nineteen-year-old skateboarder had won every amateur competition out there, and with new, bigger sponsors after him, his first X Games on the horizon, and his well-known injury and comeback headline news, he needed an agent. Bryce's biggest adversary was after him, too, but Bryce planned to come out the winner. *Win or go home*, his dad had drilled into him.

"You want to be his agent?" Honor asked, the corners of her mouth dragging down and shadowing the ray of light that seemed to follow her.

"Yes."

She swung back to her brother. "I thought you were taking things slow?"

"I'm done with slow. I'm 100 percent and now's the time. I've got this, H."

"You're not 100 percent. You'll never be 100 percent." Tension and love rang with her words, so much love Bryce felt it in the middle of chest.

"Mr. Bishop, sorry." Cooper stepped around his sister. "You don't need to hear us talk family stuff. I look forward to our meeting. I'm gonna go say hi to Sophie and Zane."

Bryce nodded. The kid had poise. And determination. After his back injury many thought he'd give up skateboarding. But athletes at his level didn't give in. They couldn't. Their sport lived in their blood and quitting wasn't an option.

He glanced at Honor after the front door shut. With her head canted down he couldn't make out how she felt, but it didn't matter. He'd give his best to Cooper, professionally and personally. He didn't know how not to be friends with his clients, even though that mentality had cost him this last year.

One of his athletes had done the unthinkable. Gotten drunk at a party and assaulted a woman. The press went crazy and the backlash had almost cost Bryce several of his other clients who didn't want to be associated with something so horrible. Bryce didn't blame them. He and Danny had dropped the asshole, and with help from a few respected friends and Bryce's father, managed to lose only two other clients. Rebuilding the Bishop-Ellis reputation was still a work in progress.

Bryce shuddered, regret and that slow burn of anger he still couldn't shake thrumming through his veins. His father's look of disappointment even as he took care of the breach of contract lawsuit thrown at Bryce and Danny still lingered, and Bryce wanted nothing more than to make his father proud. Adding a good kid like Cooper to his agency was the best way to do that.

· · ·

"Why do we have to put the seat down? Why can't women put the seat up?" Cooper said, adding his two cents to the group discussion on relationships. Honor glared at her brother from across the breakfast bar in Zane and Sophie's kitchen. He *never* put the seat down. They shared a house and many a late night run to the bathroom had her butt falling into the toilet.

"Dropping the seat takes a fraction of a second," she said, noting the guys—Bryce, Danny, Zane and Zane's brother-in-law Mark—nodded in agreement with her brother.

"True," Bryce said, "and I guess lifting the seat takes a fraction longer?"

"Lifting it takes a hand, so there's more effort involved."

"True again. And men appreciate it when a woman uses her hand." A sexy little gleam in the corners of his eyes kicked Honor's heart rate up a notch.

The guys chuckled. "Definitely," Danny said, one side of his mouth quirking up.

Sophie harrumphed. "Men need the seat down, too sometimes. Women never need it up."

Honor spewed her coffee across the counter. Everyone else cracked up. Sophie's cheeks flamed red, but Zane pulled her closer and whispered in her ear.

"Okay. Time for everyone to go," Sophie said, scooting all of them up and out. "Thanks for making this such a fun night."

The adorably happy look on Sophie's face filled Honor with a mixture of joy and longing. That second emotion got Honor to take hold of her brother and move faster than everyone else. She grabbed her bag of goodies for winning the scavenger hunt and hauled Coop out the door with a quick "bye" over her shoulder.

"Jeez, H, where's the fire?" Coop asked on their way down the driveway.

"Just hurry up. Did you walk here?" He nodded. "Me, too." As soon as they cleared the corner, she let go of his arm and slowed her steps. Took a quiet, deep inhale, the cool, crisp night air filling her lungs. Winter nights were her favorite.

"Do Mom and Dad know about the agent thing?" she asked. Their parents were celebrating their anniversary with a Sun Princess cruise and had two months left on the trip. They tried to touch base when the ship docked in port.

"Yeah, they'd gotten some calls before they left. Dad's got some hotshot from CAA he wants me to meet with next week."

"I really don't think you're ready for this. Please don't let Dad pressure you into jumping back in too soon." Honor loved her father, but sometimes he pushed Coop a little too hard.

"This isn't about you. It's about me, and I'm making the decision to move forward."

Honor put a hand on his arm to bring them to a stop. Her

stomach clenched. For almost two years he'd been fighting his way back, and she'd never been prouder. What was a little more time? "You're too young to make a decision like this on your own. How do you know these guys have your best interest? They see dollar signs and nothing else. At least wait until Dad gets back."

"I can't…" He took a deep breath. "I don't want to wait. I've been practicing non-stop, hitting the gym, and I've dominated the past three tournaments I entered. In the next month I'm getting an agent and announcing I've gone pro."

He'd been a week away from that announcement when he had his accident. Fear clambered up her spine. One wrong landing and he'd never walk again. But her brother had what she never did. Tenacity. And he refused to let one mistake beat him.

She wished she could say the same.

"I'm only looking out for you." She started walking again. With their parents a million miles away, she was responsible for her brother.

"Don't need it." He put an arm around her shoulders and smiled that lopsided grin that made girls fall all over him.

"We'll see." Agents were cutthroat, putting their professional goals above their client's well being. Or so she remembered from two years ago when a few came sniffing around her brother.

"Let's change the subject since I know how much you like to talk about yourself."

"Pfft." Coop was one of only a few people who could get her to share stuff. He didn't judge, didn't call her flighty, and could keep a secret. Unlike the rest of her small hometown.

"You got all sorts of wedding crap this weekend?"

"It's not crap." She whacked him in the stomach.

"Ow." He fake rubbed his rock hard abs like they hurt. "I can help with the store… after all the wedding crap."

Honor rolled her eyes. "That would be great. Thanks." The store was number four on Payton's list. As an event specialist for the mayor's office, Honor kept busy, but not *that* busy, and she and Pay had tossed around the idea of opening an antique store. They'd both been history majors in college and Honor loved old things—furnishings, pottery, glass, jewelry, movie memorabilia, anything from life in the past. She'd started collecting things as a kid, her eye drawn to items that looked homeless, like they didn't belong. So after Payton passed away and Honor saw "open an antique store" on her list, she'd asked her father for a loan to get started.

Occasionally things worked in her favor, and she'd grabbed the small space on Main Street that became available two months ago. In her free time she'd been working to get it ready.

"I'm crazy good with a paint brush," Cooper said, breaking into her thoughts.

"You're crazy good at everything." She put her arm around his waist and her head on his shoulder as they continued down the sidewalk.

"True. And since I'm helping you, think you could sign my name to your wedding gift for Sophie and Zane?"

"Already did."

"Sweet."

In Cooper language sweet equated to thank you. It also described her brother. He hated hearing it, and much preferred "badass," but they had each other's backs and in Honor's world that meant sweet.

They walked in silence the rest of the way to their cozy two-bedroom house across the street from the beach. Honor opened the front door and the second they went inside, peace fell over her. Nothing could touch her inside these four walls.

"'Night, H." Cooper headed down the hall to his bedroom.

"'Night." She put her gift bag on the upholstered ottoman

that served as a coffee table and plopped down on the chenille sofa, her butt so comfy in the soft fabric it wanted to divorce her and marry it. While her brother could walk into his room, climb into bed, and be asleep in under a minute, she needed a few minutes to decompress.

"I'm sorry, Pay," she whispered, thinking back to when she'd kissed Bryce. "Truly sorry."

She'd apologized to Payton more than once over the course of their friendship. They'd fought like sisters, forgave like sisters. But this apology didn't take away the stab of regret. How could it when the impossible attraction she felt for Bryce only intensified every time she saw him.

*Suck it up, girl.* The next three days were about Sophie and Zane, and she could—would—be the perfect bridesmaid. When the wedding ended, so did her time with the groomsman.

If Bryce became her brother's agent, though... That added another layer of familiarity she didn't like. Not one bit. She didn't want her brother to love him. Didn't want her parents to either. And they would. They all would. Bryce had that something that put everyone at ease and in like with him at hello.

She leaned forward and picked up the Roseville pottery book Payton had given her for her birthday. Thumbing to page one hundred, she carefully slipped out the piece of paper that held Payton's list.

Until tonight, no one else knew about the list. She'd kept it to herself so that when she failed to fulfill all five items, she'd be the only one to know.

When, not if. And it killed her.

She wasn't sure why she'd told Bryce except that it had felt nice to open up to someone who was close to Payton, too. The someone who had made what should have been easy into a tangled mess. Sharing responsibility for the screw-up made her feel a tiny bit better about it. But in the next few weeks—before *she* turned twenty-five—she'd figure out a way to follow through on her promise.

She tucked the list back inside the pages of the book, hugged the hard cover to her chest, and unfolded herself from the couch. From this moment on, she'd dedicate herself to the list and honoring Payton the best way she knew how. For once, she'd do something right.

# Chapter Three

Friday mornings meant cinnamon-flavored fried dough stuffed with gooey apple chunks and dusted with powdered sugar. Perfection otherwise known as apple fritters. How Rachel, the owner of the Beach Café, crammed so much goodness into the tiny breakfast treats, Honor didn't know, but they had to be laced with something addictive because everyone in town craved them.

Honor knew this because a hundred people stood in front of her in line. Okay, not a hundred, but enough to put her on a hungry edge since her fritter need had started well over an hour ago. She held the glass front door propped open with her foot, the delicious smell of baked bliss wafting to her nose before it drifted right out into the cool, misty air.

She also needed coffee.

Dreams of her misdeed with Bryce had interfered with all her good sleep. Leaving bad sleep. And bad feelings. She covered a yawn with her hand.

Someone waving his arm caught her attention above her fingertips.

There was a God.

She moved toward the front of the line, saying hello to everyone she passed, pausing for a second to give white-haired Mr. Case, owner of the building housing her new shop, a kiss on the cheek. She reached her favorite old guy right after that. "Uncle Tuck, hi."

"Hello, Sunshine. Thought I'd buy you breakfast." He wrapped her in a hug that made her feel six years old all over again. She hung on a little longer than necessary.

"Thank you. Good surf this morning?" His board shorts were damp and his hair smelled like saltwater. Tucker Mitchell had been one of the best pro surfers once upon a time.

"Not bad. Kicked a few of the young guys' keesters."

"I'm sure you did." Her great uncle still did aerial maneuvers that drew gasps from beachgoers.

They stepped to the counter where she ordered large everything. Seemed like a good idea considering the full day ahead. Sophie's parents and extended family were arriving later this morning, and Honor had offered to make sure everyone got settled into the White Strand Cove Inn. Then the bridesmaids had a date to pick up their dresses before everyone gathered for the rehearsal dinner.

"I hear there's a wedding this weekend," Tuck said, handing over a bag of fritters and her mountain roast coffee as they stepped away from the counter. "You still aiming to dodge that bullet?"

"You know how I feel about those bullets." Tuck wore bachelor like a badge of honor. He'd been engaged once, but the morning of the big day he'd called it off. Blamed his fickle heart and thought his fiancée deserved better. Honor understood the feeling.

He pulled on her ponytail. "Don't let your mother hear that."

"You're the only one who hears it." She took a sip from

her cup. "This is perfect. Thank you."

"You're the only chick I know who drinks her coffee black."

"Why mess with a good thing?"

"Nicely said, Padawan. You got time to sit?" He nodded to a table in the corner.

Honor opened her white paper bag and breathed in the sweet perfection. "I wish I did, but I've got to run to the shop and then do a bunch of wedding stuff."

"Hello, Tucker," Mrs. Landry said with a saucy ring in her voice. She gave a kind, genuine smile to Honor as she scooted past them.

"Morning, Evie." He reached out with his arm and…

"You did not just pinch Widow Landry's butt," Honor said, wishing she could unsee the deed. Everyone in town knew the two of them had a thing for each other, but jeez….

"You're right, I didn't. More like squeezed." The corners of his thin, weathered lips lifted high enough to reach his pale blue eyes.

"TMI, Uncle Tuck." She kissed his cheek. "Thanks for breakfast. Love you."

"Don't be a stranger," he called as she hurried out the door of the café and down the palm tree lined street.

She slowed her steps to enjoy the quiet morning and pulled her first fritter from the bag. Still early, the shops were silent, and she gazed into the windows as she walked and ate. She crossed over Bluff, glancing south to the sea, dustings of sunshine sparkling off the water a few blocks away.

Two more fritters, another block. The sun grew more insistent. A car horn sounded, drawing her attention to the street. Dylan, Cooper's best friend, waved from his beat-up convertible and shouted, "Hey, Honorlicious."

"Hey, Dylan. Keep your eyes on the road."

He saluted and she turned to watch him drive off. Duct

tape covered his right taillight and a black and white "Be Excellent to Each Other" bumper sticker with a picture of Abe Lincoln helped hide chipped paint. She smiled, dug out another fritter, this one loaded with powdered sugar, and whirled back around.

Where she collided with a hard chest, inhaled the powdered sugar, and proceeded to cough in a fit of chokehold proportions.

One big, warm hand wrapped around her upper arm. A second hand patted her back. He said something, but she couldn't make it out since she was about to hack up a lung. She knew his voice, though. And his delicious smell. His hands stayed put until she finally quieted down.

Through watery eyes, she glanced up at her roadblock. His gray T-shirt had coffee stains splattered across it. And... she sucked in her bottom lip... fan-fritter-tastic, she'd spit up on him, too.

She moved her almost-empty coffee cup to her other hand and wiped away the evidence of her spew. Mortified and at a loss for words, she kept right on rubbing his chest like a total lunatic.

And because he had a really nice chest. It distracted her from the apology that finally landed on the tip of her tongue.

"You done?" Bryce's deep, sexy voice brought her back to her senses. What the heck was she doing?

"I'm so sorry. I wasn't paying attention. I'll buy you a new shirt, or clean this one." She finally met his amused, and also very amiable, eyes. "Fritter?" She held up the bag.

"No, I'm the one who's sorry. I was reading a text and not watching where I was walking. You okay?"

"Yes."

They stared at each other for several super-charged seconds before he took the bag and looked inside. "There's only one left."

"It's all yours." No way did she plan to put any more fritter near her mouth.

He pulled the baked treat out and took a bite. She watched him like he'd been coated in powdered sugar, too, and she wanted to lick it off him. Not good. Sooo not good. She looked away, reminding herself she was behaving like the worst kind of friend.

He finished it off, crinkled the bag into a ball, and said, "Thanks."

"Sure. I, uh, guess I'll see you later at the rehearsal dinner." She stepped around him. "Have a good day."

She'd passed three stores when she felt him come up beside her. He'd either taken the minute to watch her backside or decide if he wanted more of her company. Both could only lead to trouble.

"Where you headed?" he asked.

She cringed and thought about changing directions. Unpacked boxes and a mess of inventory cluttered the antique store, and besides that, Honor liked to keep quiet about it. But since Bryce already knew about the list, she said. "To my antique store."

"Does it have something to do with Payton's list?"

Her heart hurried its beat. "Yes, but here's the thing." She tossed her coffee cup into a trashcan. "No one knows about the list. People in town know Pay and I wanted to go into business together, and I've told everyone this is to honor that dream. But if you could keep the whole list thing to yourself, I'd really appreciate it."

"My lips are sealed."

"Thanks."

"On one condition."

The small two-story building with white trim around the windows and a sloped shingle roof came into view. Honor rubbed behind her ear. She ground her teeth together. "What condition?"

"Tell me what else is on the list."

She stopped walking and without thinking jammed her finger into his chest. "You're blackmailing me to stay quiet?"

He stepped back and raised his arms, bent at the elbows, palms flat. Surrender her ass. And if he thought his cute little smile and cleft in his chin along with those dreamy, too-sharp eyes would have some affect on her, he was wrong. She wouldn't tell him another thing about Payton's wishes.

"I'd rather call it friendly persuasion," he said.

"We aren't really friends and you're about as congenial as a hippopotamus with a tooth ache." She strode away. "And forget what I said about your shirt," she called over her shoulder. Childish. But whatever.

"I'm curious, is all." He fell right back in step beside her. His interest in Payton cut to the quick, reminding her where his heart had once lay. Maybe still lay.

"When I'm interested in something I don't include stipulations. I'll be sure to mention this tactic of yours to my brother."

He flinched. "Point taken, but I thought no one else knew about the list."

She inwardly fumed because dammit, he was right. "Don't you have somewhere else to be this morning?"

He looked at the silver manly-man watch on his wrist. "Not for another half hour. And thanks to you I had a fritter and coffee, so I'm good."

She slid a glance his way. His boyish simper made her forget herself, and she had to bite the inside of her cheek to stop from giggling. From wet clothes last night to dirty ones this morning, for a serious guy, he didn't let flubs bother him.

His good humor was insanely attractive.

Honor had a feeling no matter what she said he'd find a way to stick around, so she kept quiet. She waved to Jules rounding the corner of her flower shop.

"Hi, Honor," Jules said, a big white bucket filled with bright colored flowers in her hands.

"Need help with that?" Bryce asked, his body leaning in Jules' direction.

"Nope. Thanks, though." She disappeared inside an open glass door.

Honor knelt and retrieved the key from the plastic rock in the flowerbed under the wooden stairs. Jules had been nice enough to plant some roses and maintain a small garden for her since Honor killed even fake plants.

"Honor?" Bryce said.

Key in hand, she turned. He stood really close. Too close. Her knees reacted by wobbling a little. She held herself steady with a hand to the white staircase. "Yes?"

"Tell me you don't keep the key to your store in a rock."

"Where else would I keep it?" She scooted around him and started up the stairs.

He followed. "On your person. In your purse. Somewhere it's safe?"

"I hate carrying a purse and if I put the key in my pocket, I'd lose it." She wore a striped black and white cotton-blend dress today that fell to her ankles and hugged her body in the most comfortable way. Two small pockets sat on each hip, one held a ten for the breakfast she'd been treated to, the other held lip balm. Not the end of the world if she lost either one.

"What about a car key?"

"It's under the front seat." She tossed a quick smile over her shoulder. "There are no key thieves in White Strand. The only crime that happens here is during bingo night when someone uses a black Sharpie to change a number."

She stopped at the top of the stairs and put the key in the lock. "Umm..." She turned and looked down at Bryce. He stood two steps from the top of the landing. "Thanks for the company but I'll see you later."

"I don't get to come in?"

"It's still a work in progress."

"Would it make a difference if I told you I'd really like to see what you and Payton wanted to create?" A swallow worked its way down his throat. She hadn't considered how hard it might be for him, too, to have lost Payton. Twice actually. Without any sort of conclusion but silence.

Her shoulders sagged. He deserved some breathing room and consideration. "I sometimes forget she's not here. Is that weird?"

"No." He took a step up. "I think that's perfectly normal. I remember when my grandfather passed away and my dad telling me he still expected him to walk through the door. And on several occasions my dad even picked up the phone to call him before remembering he was gone."

"How old were you?"

"Eleven."

"I'm sorry. Do you remember him?"

"A few things here and there."

"I wish all the time Payton was still here." Honor turned and opened the door in silent invitation. Bryce softened things inside her, and while having Payton in common hurt too much for anything serious to happen between them, maybe they could let each other off the hook now and then.

"She's lucky to have had a friend like you."

Honor squeezed her eyes shut. "I'm the lucky one," she said under her breath.

Sunlight spilled into the space and she hurried over to the windows to let in some fresh air. Turning to find Bryce scanning the large room, she almost changed her mind and asked him to leave. The far left wall cried out for new paint. The hardwood floor needed a few new boards and sanding, and once she found the right screwdriver, she'd assemble the pile of shelves.

Several pieces of furniture decorated the space, but boxes overflowing with fragile items wrapped in newspaper sat in no particular order in the corners.

"It's nice," he said, his voice sincere, and her overactive nerves calmed. "Is the space below yours, too?"

"Only until Mr. Case rents it. For now he's letting me store a few things for free."

Bryce raised his eyebrows. "You're leaving something out."

How did he know that? "Okay, not exactly free. I'm helping him get a date with Shirley in the mayor's office."

"How's that going?"

She lifted some loose papers on the small desk in the middle of the room. "Have you ever tried getting two stubborn senior citizens together?"

He came up beside her. "Can't say that I have. You looking for something?"

"My measuring tape." She searched the desk drawer to no avail. "I wanted to measure one of the walls."

"We could do it the old fashioned way with our feet. I'm a size eleven, so that'll get you a pretty close measurement. Which wall?" He wandered over to the help-me-I-need-paint wall.

"That's the one," she managed to get out, her mind having immediately jumped to shoe size indicating another size. Or was it big hands that meant a big—

"Back me up here, shop owner." He gestured her over with a lift and tilt of his chin.

She hustled to his side while she extinguished all thoughts of inches and how she'd felt him pressed up against her their night in his hotel room.

"You all right? You look a little flush."

"Fine." She glanced down with every intention of looking

at his feet, but got stuck on his zipper instead. Involuntary and sooo inconvenient, given he cleared his throat. Her gaze jumped back to his handsome face.

His very nice white teeth sparkled. Crap. He'd caught her checking out his junk. This man discombobulated her from here until Tuesday.

"Like what you see?"

"I don't know what you're talking about." She kept eye contact, daring him to call her bluff.

"I could show you."

She shook her head. They couldn't flirt and keep the tenuous connection they'd just established. "No. You can't."

"You're right." He pressed a hand to the wall and looked down. "Sorry. I forgot myself for a minute."

"It's okay. I did, too." Turning off the feelings he triggered whenever he stood close hadn't been as easy as she'd hoped it would be. "So, measurement?"

"Let's do it."

With silent agreement, they focused on his shoes and she quietly kept track of each step he took along the wall.

"Fifty-seven," he said at the same time she said, "Fifty-three." She'd let his very nice counting voice intrude on her thoughts for a couple of seconds, but she thought she'd stayed with him.

"One of us can't count," he teased before his attention drifted and he veered around her to pick something up off the floor. "Look what I found." He held up the tape measure.

She snagged it from him. "Five bucks says I'm closer."

"You're on."

They worked together to take the measurement, Bryce hanging on to the metal dispenser while she pulled the tape. "Sixty-two," she said, letting go and watching it fire back into its case.

Bryce gave a small victory smile. He put the tape measure

on a box marked "Roseville" in messy black marker and strode toward her. "Tell you what, keep the five and tell me about that." He nodded toward the small square pillow sitting on the window ledge that Payton had made for her.

Happy surprise filled her at his notice. She sighed. "It's beautiful and awful at the same time, isn't it?" A five year-old boy, hands caked with mud, sewed better than Payton.

"Is that supposed to be a butterfly on there?" Bryce followed her toward the window.

"Yes." Honor picked up the unskillful gift she loved more than anything. "Payton made it for me."

"With her eyes closed?"

"We both know she was about as artistic as a baboon." She glanced up at him. "A really pretty baboon." His blank expression threw the beat of her heart off for a second. Maybe he didn't know that about her. "Anyway, I thought it should have a home here."

"The saying underneath the butterfly is familiar."

*You're my estate*, it said. "It's taken from Emily Dickinson. Her quote goes, 'My friends are my estate.' I'm surprised you recognized it."

"My sister is big on literature."

Honor nodded. She didn't know he had a sister.

"Payton told me you were the most important person in her life."

"Until she met you."

He shrugged. "I don't think so. If she was as committed to me as I was to her, then I would have been with her until the end, too."

Bryce's pained expression was like a hundred poison arrows to her heart. She knew he valued relationships. Payton had shared that he'd had several girlfriends before her. Nothing too serious, but he liked commitment. He didn't do things halfway or without care. Another reason he was completely off limits to a girl like her.

The only thing Honor had committed to was tying her Nike's. And that was because she'd tripped over the damn laces one too many times when left undone.

She had selfish bones she wasn't proud of.

Even if she wanted to get to know Bryce better, she couldn't. She'd fail him, just like she did everything else, and she hated the thought of failing something so good.

Lance flashed through her mind. Her high school boyfriend had wanted forever with her. A year behind him in school, they'd been together a year when his Senior Prom arrived. "I've got a very important question to ask you tonight," he'd told her the morning of the big party. She'd silently freaked out. She was only seventeen and while she loved Lance in her own way, she didn't love him the way he wanted. His proposal—she *knew* that was the question— loomed over her with a death grip on her chest all day and when the time came to go to prom with him, she couldn't do it. She bailed and went for a drive down the coast with Bobby Gibbs. Bobby was only a friend, there to lend support, but her selfish action had hurt Lance. Rather than talk to him like she should have, she'd taken the coward's way out.

The next day Lance hurt himself.

"You're not a commitment kind of girl," Lance said when she visited him in the hospital. "Deep down I knew that... you're no good, Honor, not to anyone."

She'd nodded her agreement as he continued to insult her and then she'd left, hating herself and what she'd done.

"Honor?" Bryce's voice broke into her recollection and brought her back to the present.

"I need to go," she said, putting the pillow down and sidestepping around him. She hated hearing concern in his voice. Hated that he may have seen something on her face she didn't want him to see. Eager to get out of his reach, she tripped over a broken floorboard and fell to her hands and knees. "Dammit." Pain stung her kneecaps.

Bryce's warm touch wrapped around her arms. He lifted her up. "You okay?"

"Fine." She shrugged out of his hold, but the flash of comfort his gentle grasp elicited lingered. "Just have a ton of things to do today." The first of which included putting as much space as possible between her and the man who stirred up way too many unwelcome emotions.

• • •

Honor's unrestrained laugh drew Bryce's attention for the tenth time. He couldn't stop keeping track of everything she did. Meet his gaze from the other end of the L-shaped dining table? Four times. Twirl her finger in her hair? Five times. Smile at something the guy sitting next to her—Drew, Mark's brother—said? One time too many.

The sound of silverware striking a glass broke into his calculations and drew his attention. Zane stood up.

His best friend cleared his throat. "Thank you all for being here tonight and this weekend." A visible swallow made its way down Zane's throat before he glanced down at his bride-to-be and took Sophie's hand in his. "I never imagined I was good enough to find this kind of love and happiness, but somehow this amazing, beautiful woman decided I was worth something. She's taught me so much these past six months and I think I've taught her a few things, too." Sophie blushed. "For the rest of my life she's stuck with me and every single day she'll know what a gift she is." Sophie stood, kissed his cheek, and whispered something in his ear.

And no damn way. Zane's cheeks actually reddened. Bryce smiled. Throw every adjective at his friend—infatuated, enamored, captivated, mad about, hot for—and Zane had it ten times worse.

"Thanks for celebrating with us," Zane said. "We're both really happy to be surrounded by family and friends as we take this next step. Dinner dismissed." With that he lifted Sophie into his arms and marched out of the private dining room to hoots and hollers.

"Thought it would be you for sure," Danny said from beside him.

"What?"

"The first of us to get married. It was supposed to be you. We all knew that. Then surf stud goes and surprises us."

"Want to get drunk?" Throwing back a few seemed like a good way to forget that yeah, Bryce had thought that, too.

"Sounds good."

They wandered out of the room and headed straight for the bar of the restaurant. The Happy Harpoon had a definite happy vibe going on this evening with loud conversation at all the tables and a crowded bar. He and Danny snagged the last two barstools.

"Two vodka tonics," Bryce told the bartender.

"I'll have the same," Danny said.

Bryce shot his friend a puzzled look. "Dude."

"What? You said drunk didn't you? I'm just saving us some time." Something had been on Danny's mind for a while now, their ordeal with that bastard of a client aside, but hell if he'd share it.

Bryce would find out what it was eventually. Right now they didn't need to talk. Just drink.

The bartender deposited their order. "To Zane and Sophie." Bryce lifted his glass and clinked tumblers with Danny. "To Zane and Sophie," Danny echoed.

At the other end of the curved bar Julia, Mark, Honor, and Drew took a spot just vacated.

"When's the meeting with Cooper?" Danny asked after

a few sips. As business partners, Bryce acquired their clients and managed everything except the financial and legal facets of their athletes' careers.

"Next week. You know the guy's unbelievable. And on top of his skill he's got a good head on his shoulders. I think we'll do right by him."

"He's also Honor's brother. That going to be a problem?"

"No."

"You sure?" Danny shook his glass so the ice clinked. "They're close."

"What makes you say that?" Bryce let his gaze drift casually down the bar. Drew had his arm draped across the back of Honor's barstool and his body leaned toward hers.

"It was pretty obvious last night. She's protective. And she doesn't want him going pro."

"That's understandable given his accident. But we look out for our athletes." He tightened the grip on his glass. Honor could trust them with her brother. The idea that she didn't rankled. Did it circle back to Payton mistrusting him?

"Maybe we should let Coop go and focus on someone else."

Bryce stared at his friend. There wasn't anyone else out there Bryce was even remotely interested in, and Danny knew it. After the shitstorm they'd been through the past year, they needed someone exactly like Cooper Mitchell. Young, good upbringing, positive attitude, a comeback kid, just like they were trying to be.

"No."

Danny kept his eyes on his drink. "Okay. But if it looks like you can't handle it, I'm putting a stop to it."

"What does that mean?"

"Payton wrecked you man, and now you're after her best friend's brother. Seems to me Cooper might make life more difficult for you, not easier."

Bryce let that sink in before letting the burn of alcohol slide down his throat and his attention wander back to Honor. She had her arm propped up on the bar, her cheek in her hand and her focus on whatever Drew was saying.

"I could sit in on the meeting." Danny said.

"Fine. I don't want you worrying that pretty head of yours." Danny glared at him.

"Bye, Midge. Everything was great." Above all the voices in the busy restaurant, Bryce heard Honor's. He looked over his shoulder to see her hugging the owner of the establishment before walking out the door, Drew at her side.

Bryce turned back around. He ignored his tense shoulder muscles and glanced down the bar to where Honor had sat. Something small and shiny gleamed atop the counter. She'd told him she hated carrying a purse, but it looked like tonight she'd brought one—and forgotten about it. He jumped to his feet.

"Dude, I'll be back in a few."

Bryce grabbed the purse before he could talk himself out of it and hurried out the door. The crisp night air slapped him in the cheeks, reminding him to slow his hasty steps so as not to seem too eager to catch up with her.

A flash of yellow caught his eye from the sidewalk. Honor's strapless dress clung to her torso before falling from her waist to her ankles in a soft, loose, almost sheer material. She looked like a goddess sent from the sun to shine on everyone. Drew lifted his arm and angled it toward the back of her shoulders.

"Honor!"

She twisted around. "Is everything okay?" Lines creased her forehead as she stepped toward him.

"I think this is yours?" Bryce held up the silver bag.

More than forgetfulness flashed in her pretty eyes. Relief did, too. She held his gaze like an invisible string had them hooked together. "Yep. That's mine." A small impish grin put a twinkle in her eye.

"And Drew, Julia's looking for you. It seemed pretty urgent."

"I just said good-bye to her."

Bryce shrugged.

"It's okay," Honor said when Drew gazed at her with disappointment. "We can talk tomorrow."

"I'd like that." Drew leaned forward in a move to kiss Honor's cheek.

Only Bryce's arm and the small purse in his hand accidentally, but not really, blocked his attempt. "Sorry, dude. Your clutch, Honor." Bryce held it up in front of her. He only knew the word 'clutch' because of his grandmother.

Drew frowned and backed away.

"Goodnight," Honor called out. Then to him she said with a soft voice, "'Night," before turning and walking down the sidewalk.

He caught her elbow before she'd taken more than a few steps. "Are you walking home?"

"Yes."

"It's," he glanced at his watch, "nine o'clock."

She shrugged out of his hold and continued on her way. "The Boogeyman doesn't come out until ten, so I'm good." The humor in her voice made it impossible to let her go.

"I still can't let you walk home alone." He matched her strides.

"I thought we'd already established what a safe town I live in." She spoke to the concrete, her head tipped down and away from him. He got the feeling she didn't want him to see how much she liked his good manners.

Not that manners had much to do with his walking her home. He pulled out his phone to text Danny he wouldn't be back.

"True, but my mom raised me better than to let Boogeyman Bait tempt fate."

She giggled and looked at him out of the corner of her eye. "All right. But only because I don't want to disappoint your mom."

He slipped off his sports coat and put it around her bare shoulders. "Thank you," she whispered.

The trip took about fifteen minutes. They didn't talk, but the silence felt nice. He fought the urge to pick up her hand when their fingers brushed.

"Here I am." She stopped in front of a small Spanish Colonial style house with a small brick porch. The plum-colored front door beckoned visitors inside with understated warmth. "Thanks for the escort."

"Any time." He shoved his hands into the pockets of his slacks.

She lifted a hand to her shoulder, to pull off his jacket he guessed, but instead she stilled as they stared at each other. Under the light of the moon her eyes took on the hue of the evening sky. Breathtaking. Unforgettable.

In the distance he heard the faint drone of a television. The scent of firewood reached his nose. She dropped her gaze, sliding it down his chest to his stomach, his legs, and then slowly back up again. Her open perusal made him hard and he cursed the effect she had on him. Why did she have to be Payton's best friend and Cooper's sister? He could deny it over and over again, but the truth was he wanted to finish what they'd started. Nothing serious, just some fun.

Her naturally pink lips parted a fraction.

Despite the fact that they stood in her quaint neighborhood with little space between the houses, he'd swear nothing else existed but the two of them.

"Something on your mind?" he asked. Tell me I am, he thought. Tell me this tangled attraction goes both ways.

Possession, affection, necessity, all swam through his veins as he stared at Honor's expressive face. She tried to hide, but he saw how much he affected her even when she didn't want him to.

"Just the usual. Here you go." She handed him his jacket. "Thanks again."

"Wait. Do you have a minute?"

She gave a small, confused shake of her head. "I guess so."

"I've got to give the best man speech. Maybe you could tell me what you think." Where the hell had that come from? *You don't want to say good-night.*

Damn if that little voice inside his head hadn't decided to take over his common sense. He wanted nothing to do with her. He wanted everything to do with her.

And so he'd take a few more minutes.

"Oh. Okay." A cold breeze picked up wisps of her hair. Her body shook and she crossed her arms over her chest.

Bryce put his coat back around her.

"Why don't you come inside for a minute and give it to me?"

He couldn't help but let his dirty mind picture a few ways he'd like to give it to her. His inappropriate thoughts must have shown on his face because her cheeks reddened and she added, "The speech. You can give me your speech."

Without waiting for him to answer, she pulled the lapel of his jacket tighter and led him into her house. "Have a seat." She nodded to her couch in the small open space. "I'll be right back. I need something warm to drink. Can I get you anything?"

"I'll have whatever you're having."

He watched her enter the kitchen before he sat. One word best described her home — cozy. Wood flooring, comfortable furnishings, rich-colored paintings decorating the walls. On the fireplace mantle sat three framed photographs. Her and Cooper. Cooper with an older couple Bryce assumed were their parents. And one with her and Payton, huge smiles on their faces, the ocean behind them. Seeing the two of them together nearly cut off the oxygen supply to his lungs. This was a bad idea, being in her home, because the person he was most drawn to in that photo wasn't the woman he'd loved.

A book on the ottoman caught his eye and he picked it up to distract himself. His mom loved Roseville pottery and had a large collection of the American made designs. "You like Roseville?" he called out.

"Yes," Honor answered, glancing over at him from the kitchen counter. She gave a barely there smile as she slipped his jacket off and hung it over the back of a chair before turning back to her task.

Bryce thumbed through the glossy pages of the book. About to set it back on the ottoman, he froze when the next page he turned to carried a note tucked into the spine so it wouldn't fall out.

The beige parchment paper the size of a postcard had a list written on it in neat cursive writing that he recognized as Payton's.

*1) Have a one night stand*

*2) Get a tattoo*

*3) Take a hot air balloon ride*

*4) Open an antique store with my best friend*

*5) Fall in love*

He read it again, his stomach clenching in melancholy. Once again he wondered when she'd written it. She'd wanted a tattoo? Seemed very unlike the woman he'd known.

"What are you doing?" Honor's voice shook with distress as she put two coffee cups down on the tray atop the ottoman. "No one ever looks in that book."

He looked up to see a flash of pain fill her eyes so fast he felt it like a stake through his heart.

She grabbed the book off his lap. "You need to go."

"Honor—"

"Now." She rushed to grab his jacket, thrust it at him, and opened the front door.

"I didn't mean to—"

"Now," she repeated, her voice cracking, her bottom lip trembling. It killed him to see her so upset. The second he stepped onto the porch the door slammed shut.

"Mr. Bishop? What are you doing here?"

Bryce blinked his eyes into focus. "Cooper, hey. I walked your sister home from the rehearsal dinner."

Cooper frowned. "You're not into her are you? Because my skateboarding and my family are two things that do not overlap."

"I hear you. I was just doing a good deed, being that we're both part of the wedding party." Cooper's firm opinion knocked some sense back into him. Time to think about his agency, not the bridesmaid that had his sex drive back in full throttle. "What are you up to?"

"Getting home from my friend Dylan's house. His parents like to feed me."

Bryce scraped his hand along his jaw. "You live here?"

"Yeah." He stepped up onto the porch and put his hand on the door handle. "I'll see you at the wedding. Thanks for making sure Honor got back okay."

"Sure thing," Bryce said, the words ringing hollow. His world had never felt smaller and he didn't feel sure about anything.

# Chapter Four

"You guys are spoiling me," Sophie said, a glow on her face. She sat on the edge of the guest bedroom bed hugging the short, cozy pink sweater robe to her body. "Thank you."

"Every bride needs an official getting ready robe," Julia said.

"Especially because from the moment you wake up tomorrow you're going to be photographed," Sophie's cousin and maid of honor, Emma said. "The moms are planning to capture everything."

Sophie scrunched up her nose. "I'm happy my mom and Zane's mom like each other so much, but they're like a tag team from *My Fair Wedding*.

Honor bounced onto the bed next to Sophie. "That's better than a tag team from *Bridezillas*."

"True. I can't believe I'm getting married in twenty-four hours." Sophie glanced over at the wedding dress hanging on the back of the guest bath door. Honor kept looking at the simple, but elegant gown with beading on the bodice, too.

"Believe it, Fifi." Emma gave Sophie a quick hug. "And

you're going to be the prettiest bride ever, ever, ever. Now finish up in here while Julia and I go pick up dinner."

"Take one of the guys with you," Sophie said. She and Zane had planned a casual dinner for the wedding party and a couple of Zane's friends from out of town.

"Stop worrying. We've got it," Emma said as she and Julia left the room, closing the door behind them.

Honor stood. "Okay, let's finish packing your suitcase and then we'll make sure you've got everything ready for the big day."

Sophie laid the robe to the side and got up. Her arms wrapped tightly around Honor. "Thank you so much."

"You don't need to thank me, Soph." Honor squeezed her friend back. "I'm happy and honored to be a part of this."

"I do need to thank you." Sophie pulled back. "If it wasn't for you I wouldn't be here right now."

"What are you talking about?"

"Zane wouldn't have noticed me if it wasn't for your help and encouragement. From the minute you met me, you took me under your wing, and I'll never forget how kind you were. You're the first true friend I've ever had and I love you."

"I love you, too." Honor embraced her again. "And Zane so would have noticed you. He's a smart guy."

"Thank you for saying that." Sophie smiled and moved to the dresser to pull a small wrapped box out of the top drawer. "This is for you. Just a little something extra to tell you how special you are to me."

"Soph. You didn't need to do that."

"I know. Open it."

Honor tore into the token of friendship that meant more to her than she could say. When she saw what lay inside the box, emotion clogged the back of her throat. A silver bracelet with an infinity charm. She and Payton had worn similar bracelets as a symbol of their forever friendship. Honor had tucked both away when Pay died.

Staring at the piece of jewelry now, she blinked several times. She'd lost Payton and been given Sophie a few months later. No one could ever replace Pay, but maybe the universe *was* looking out for her.

"I love it. Thank you." She took the bracelet out of the box and put it on.

"You're welcome." Sophie beamed and twirled to her suitcase. "Now let's finish this up so I can mark it off Emma's checklist. She'll have my butt if we're not done before she gets back."

"She does like cracking the whip," Honor said. "But that's because she wants everything to be perfect for you."

"I know. But all I need is Zane."

Honor sighed. Everyone could feel the love Sophie and Zane had for each other. "Then let's speed this up so we can have a celebratory drink."

Sophie raised her eyebrows.

"I promise it will go down so smooth, you'll want a second one." Honor had been there for Sophie's first alcoholic drink and well, spewing had been involved.

"You still might want to keep your distance," Sophie joked.

It only took a few minutes to finish Sophie's packing and line up all her wedding day accessories. They went downstairs and found Zane's friend Aiden in the kitchen.

"Hi Aiden. Where is everyone?" Sophie asked.

"On the beach. They'll be back in a few." He moved his attention to Honor, his gaze keeping for longer than casual interest. The other night he'd tucked toilet paper where it didn't need to be tucked, too.

"That means you two get the first shots." Honor grabbed the stuff she'd brought earlier to make drinks for everyone.

Aiden moved to her side, his arm deliberately brushing

hers. "Need some help?"

"How are you with a knife?"

He grinned. "I'm good with everything." She just bet he was.

"Cut these lemons for me?" She put the produce bag in front of him. While he got busy cutting, she combined vodka and hazelnut liqueur and shook up the first batch of chocolate cake shots. She poured sugar into a bowl to dip the lemons in.

The three of them chatted and joked until Honor had three shot glasses lined up in a row. "Okay, so you drink this, then follow it up by sucking on the sugared lemon, and it tastes exactly like chocolate cake."

"Seriously?" Sophie said.

"Yes. You ready?" Honor picked up her shot. "On three." Sophie and Aiden lifted their cups in one hand and a slice of lemon in the other. "One, two, three."

"Holy heavens! Chocolate cake is in my mouth," Sophie trumpeted when finished.

"What's in your mouth?" Zane said, his voice echoing off the walls. He, Bryce, Danny, Mark, and two other surf friends of Zane's entered the kitchen.

Bryce locked eyes with hers.

Sophie spun around and wrapped her arms around Zane's neck. "Taste." And he did, with a kiss that lasted until Danny cleared his throat. At least she thought it was Danny since Bryce had her caught with his dangerous, dark eyes.

Aiden angled his head down so his mouth almost grazed her ear. "I'm all for taste tests in case you were wondering."

Honor blinked free of Bryce and turned to look at Aiden. "I wasn't, but I might be now," she whispered. Aiden had one night stand written all over him.

"We need another round," Sophie declared, spurring Honor back into action.

Grateful for the task, she kept her focus on drink making,

all too aware that not only were Aiden's eyes on her, but Bryce's, too.

"Antiques, special events, bartender, you're a woman of many talents," Bryce said a few minutes later, his voice slipping over her warmer than the shot that had slid down her throat.

"I owe this one to my friend Cambria. She works as a bartender for a party planning company and taught me how to make it. Did you like it?"

"I did." He stood near enough that his minty, spicy, pure male scent surrounded her.

"Want another?"

"I'm good. Listen, about last night—"

"Don't worry about it," she rushed out under her breath. She didn't want to talk about Payton's list in a kitchen full of people. It infuriated her that he'd seen it. But really, it was her own stupid fault for keeping the list in the book. She'd worried she'd lose it otherwise, just like she lost every other note or reminder. Of course she had the list memorized, but having that piece of paper was like having a piece of her best friend and she'd wanted to keep it. Maybe Bryce didn't deserve her anger, but she suffered it all the same.

"Okay, how many shots do I need to catch up?" Emma said at the top of her voice. She and Julia strode into the kitchen with pizza boxes and brown bags Honor knew held salad, garlic bread, and spaghetti and meatballs inside them.

For the next hour everyone ate and talked, sitting and standing wherever comfortable in the large kitchen. Bryce made no attempt to talk to her again, or get close enough for her to smell him, but their eyes did meet a few times across the room.

And each time she felt an uninvited flutter in the pit of her stomach.

Once everyone had finished and the kitchen was cleaned,

the guys headed to the White Strand Inn. The girls were sleeping over with Sophie.

"I don't think I'm going to get a wink of sleep tonight," Sophie said, curled up on the couch in the living room. She wore her *Beach Bride* pajama set.

Honor, Julia and Emma wore their matching *Beach Bridesmaid* jammies. "Warm milk," Emma said. "Isn't that what they say?"

"With cookies," Julia added.

"Oh no!" Sophie leaned forward. "I forgot to give Bryce the note I wrote to Zane."

"What note?" Emma asked.

"Julia gave me the idea. I wrote Zane a love note and I need one of the guys to slip it to him right before the ceremony."

"That is so sweet." Emma sighed.

Sophie stood. "I hate to ask this, but would one of you mind running it over to the hotel? I'm afraid I'll forget tomorrow."

"If I go I might not come back," Julia said. "This is the first night I'm away from my new hubby and I miss him."

"I may not return either," Emma said, her voice taking on a coquettish tone. "Bryce is totally hot and I might—"

"I'll do it," Honor interrupted, hoping she sounded like she was doing everyone a favor and not at all bothered by Emma's admission. Because she wasn't.

Not at all.

• • •

The Kings were tied with two minutes to go, but Bryce couldn't concentrate on the big screen TV in the lounge at the inn. The other guys stayed absorbed in the action, but with Aiden sitting next to him all Bryce could think about was how the guy had flirted with Honor all night.

"Ohhhh!" Several people shouted at what Bryce guessed was a missed shot on goal.

The one time he'd gotten close to Honor, she'd smelled like gardenias, woman, and chocolate and he'd wanted to breathe her in until morning.

More yells and a few curse words rounded the room. Abruptly Aiden stood and said, "Hey."

"And here I thought I'd find you guys having a pillow fight in Zane's suite."

Bryce swung his head in surprise at the sweet, sexy voice. Honor stood next to Aiden wearing pink and white striped pajama pants and a pink long sleeved shirt with *Beach Bridesmaid* written across the chest.

Aiden whispered something in her ear.

She tilted her chin to the side and gave him a small smile. Bryce's hands clenched.

Zane jumped to his feet. "Is everything okay?" Worry tainted his normally upbeat voice. "Is Sophie all right?"

"She's fine. Everything is good. I was sent over to talk to Bryce for a minute."

At mention of his name, Bryce connected with Honor's remarkable eyes. He pushed his chair back and an absurd amount of pleasure filled his chest when he stood above Aiden. "Should we go somewhere private?"

"Yes."

Shouts erupted in the lounge and everyone leapt to their feet. Bryce glanced at the TV. The Kings had scored with ten seconds left in the period.

Aiden put his hand on Honor's arm and said something Bryce couldn't hear.

She did one of the those slow blinks women do when they're flattered. Her lips pressed together in a barely-there smile.

Bryce ground his teeth together. Was she seriously considering whatever Aiden had said to her? Of course she was. This was her chance for a wedding hook-up. He shouldn't care one way or the other what she crossed off Payton's list. But if the tightness in his gut was any indication, he did.

With her eyes cast downward, she whispered in Aiden's ear. Bryce stared at her mouth trying to read her lips, and because their pink color drew him like a wrestler to the mat. Ready to take down the guy that might catch her interest.

Not his business, he reminded himself.

Aiden nodded and Honor waved her arm in a motion for Bryce to follow. She walked through the lobby and out the sliding glass door to the pool area. Landscape lighting lit the area in soft yellow and the pool, bathed in white light, gave off a turquoise glow.

They stood near the edge, Honor drawn to the water in a way he recognized from athletes who'd spent time swimming.

"You swim?" he asked.

"I used to."

"I'm pretty sure swimming is like riding a bike. You don't forget how to do it."

She gave him a side glare. "If this agent thing doesn't work out for you, you could be a comedian."

He winced. She had no idea how close he'd come to losing his agent gig last year. The thought sobered his unrelenting attraction to her. "You wanted to talk to me about something?" His clipped tone left no room for any more ribbing.

A groove drew her eyebrows together. She handed him a neatly folded piece of paper he hadn't noticed she held. Their fingers brushed and he had the urge to grab her hand and bring her flush against him. "Sophie asked me to give this to you. It's a note to Zane and she'd like you to give it to him right before the ceremony."

Bryce looked briefly down at the note. "Did you read it?"

"Of course not. And you'd better not either. It's private."

"Got it. Tell Sophie I'll be sure he gets it."

"Thanks." She swayed like she couldn't decide if she wanted to stay or go. "See you tomorrow."

"You going back to the house?" Jesus. His mouth had entirely disconnected from his brain.

"Where else would I go?"

He shrugged. If he opened his mouth again who knew what would come out. Honor made him completely forget himself.

She studied him like she held a magnifying glass up to his head and was seconds away from discovering every detail inside his gray matter. A smile bloomed across her face. Yep. Seconds. "You're wondering if I'm going to meet Aiden."

"The guy's had more hookups than a global satellite."

Honor cracked up. "Sounds like he'd be perfect then. The last thing I want is a relationship."

"It is?" he asked surprised.

Further down the patio a couple of teenage boys joked around and tossed a football across the pool, running and bouncing around the perimeter.

"Payton wanted the white picket fence. I don't. But just so you know," she leaned closer, "I told Aiden no thanks. Not because I wasn't tempted, but because…"

Somehow Bryce had moved closer, too, and little space separated him from Honor under lights nestled in the palm trees around them.

"Because?"

"Because the girls are waiting for me." She gazed at the glass surface of the pool. "Besides, he's staying in town for a few extra days so there's still time to make something happen. If I want."

In his periphery, Bryce noticed one of the teenage boys had gotten closer to where he stood. Two seconds later, the football came flying, its trajectory in perfect line with Honor's unsuspecting face.

"Look out!" Unthinking, Bryce pushed Honor out of harm's way. And right into the swimming pool.

She cursed and landed in the water with a large splash.

Bryce shot his arm out and caught the football with one hand. The kid across the pool shouted "sorry" while the other one apologized more than once as he retrieved the ball from Bryce.

Honor broke the surface of the water, reached for the edge, and scowled up at him. "What was that?" she demanded.

"Sorry, lady," the kid said. "My friend threw the football at you by mistake."

Her attention moved to the teen. "Oh. I didn't …" she trailed off and looked back at Bryce. "It's okay."

Bryce kept his eyes on Honor's and knelt, vaguely aware of the boy running off. "How's the water?"

"Tango keeps it heated so it's not bad."

"I'm sorry. Probably should have intercepted instead of shoved." Damn, she looked pretty wet. His thoughts raced back to them getting caught in the sprinklers and how he'd wanted to kiss her.

"Quick thinking isn't one of your virtues, huh?"

Back to the teasing and he liked it. "Guess not." At least not where she was concerned. She tossed every thread of logic he possessed into complete disarray.

"Help me out?" She gave him her hand.

He took it and catching him off guard, she pulled him right into the water, head over feet. Her laughter rang in his ear as he went under.

"Oops," she said when he popped to the surface. Her grin was about the best shape of happy he'd ever had the pleasure of being close to. "You really should have seen that coming."

"Goes back to that quick thinking thing." He made like he

was swimming toward the concrete edge, but instead grabbed her by the waist and tugged her under.

Then he kicked away from her, treading water in the middle of the deep end. His clothes made it a little tougher than usual to keep afloat, but he managed. Honor sputtered and flailed when she came up for air. She sent him a man-eating glare, said "This is war," and swam straight for him.

He backstroked out of her reach, but the girl *could* swim. She caught his ankle and pulled him under.

Twisting and swimming full tilt, he made it to the shallow end before he let her catch him again. She palmed his shoulders and pressed down but he didn't budge. She tried again, lifting out of the water this time. Her shirt clung to her skin, giving him a view of her rounded breasts and pert nipples. His mouth watered.

He wanted to touch and lick and suck and see if her breasts were as sensitive as he'd imagined they were since getting a quick preview all those months ago.

So lost in thoughts of her sexy body, he didn't see the splash coming. Water went up his nose. He choked and coughed before wiping the smirk off her face with his own splash.

They paddled water at each other like two kids until a very loud, very deep, "*Ahem*," caught their attention.

Tango, ex-NFL linebacker and owner of the inn loomed above them, thick arms crossed over his chest. "Pool hours are over you two." He walked away, towels on the ground where he'd stood.

Bryce looked at Honor at the same time she looked at him and they burst into laughter. He couldn't remember the last time he'd laughed so free and easy with a woman. Like nothing else mattered at the moment.

She swam to the side. He followed, reality hitting him as the one big flaw in this escapade set in.

"We've got a problem," he said, coming up beside her.

"We do?" The lilt of her cheerful voice hinted at other shenanigans and he wanted to know what other mischief she'd gotten into.

He took the note from Sophie out of his pocket and placed it on the ground.

"Oh, crapity, crap, crap," Honor muttered. Her lids briefly closed, her shoulders dropped. "It's my fault. Hopefully Sophie doesn't mind writing another one and I'll get it to you tomorrow."

"Partners in crime, Honor. Tell Sophie I'm just as much to blame."

Soft, surprised eyes met his, like no one had shared blame with her before. And her quiet nod of thanks knocked the wind right out of him.

Whatever he thought he saw there, though, he was wrong. They weren't on the same team. And never would be. He'd been abandoned and blindsided by the opposite sex and reminded himself to choose his words more carefully. Because from now on *he* planned to be the love-them-and-leave-them type, not the other way around

# Chapter Five

Honor wiped away a tear slipping out of the corner of her eye. The vows Sophie and Zane said to each other spoke of amazing love and devotion, and the way Zane looked at his bride made Honor feel like she'd intruded on an intimate moment. She wanted to look away. She couldn't look away. Her heart rejoiced and yearned at the same time.

They couldn't have asked for a more beautiful evening on the beach. Hurricane lamps cast a warm glow, light blue surfboards that said *Now and Forever* held up the canopy the bridal party stood under. With the ocean as inspiration, the wedding coordinator had drawn from its colors and used sea glass as the decorative foundation to make everything in and around Zane and Sophie's house look like an underwater paradise. Different sized blue and green glass balls from fisherman's nets were strung around the site, and when they caught the flicker from the hurricane lamps, it was magical.

The pastor told a joke about a minister, a surfer, and a beautiful redhead walking into a bar and everyone chuckled. Pastor Michael was about as laid back as they came. He'd even surfed with Zane this morning. Right now, he smiled that warm, you-can-tell-me-all-your-problems smile and declared Zane and Sophie husband and wife.

Amid loud applause from the fifty or so guests, Zane gave Sophie a sweeping kiss before taking her hand and leading her down the sand toward their house.

Honor quickly swiped at another rebellious tear, stepped forward, and took Bryce's arm to follow the procession. Of course she'd been paired with the too-handsome groomsman.

And the man her best friend had said she could see herself marrying. Their romance may have been private and a whirlwind, but Payton always came home from weekends with Bryce with stars in her eyes and her heart full of devotion. Bryce had been committed to Pay. Had he thought about forever with her, too? Honor's breath caught. Payton had been taken in the blink of an eye instead of getting the chance to say, "I do." Honor ached to throw fairness the middle finger, but wrapped her hand tighter around her bouquet instead.

"Nice ceremony," Bryce said. "You look really pretty."

She didn't want him to say nice things to her. After the playful time they'd had in the pool last night, and his kind parting words, her defenses were crumbling. She did love her floor length sea green sheath dress, though, so said, "Thank you. You look very handsome." In navy dress slacks and a white button down with the top button open and the sleeves pushed up to his elbows, he got her vote for sexiest groomsman on the planet.

She bit down on her lip. Not for the first time today he stared at her mouth.

Since they'd taken pictures earlier, they were swept right into the house for champagne and appetizers. Honor had never seen Sophie look so vibrant, so happy. Lively conversation and laughter filled the beach house. Soft music played from a sound system.

Honor put down her half-filled glass of bubbly and snuck into the kitchen. "Hey, Elena."

"Honor. Hi. You look gorgeous. Do not come too close. If anything gets on that dress I'll never forgive myself." Elena was one of the best private chefs on the west coast. On either coast, actually.

"That shrimp prosciutto appetizer was to die for. And you know I can't get enough of your mini duck tacos." She gave a little wave to the two women helping Elena prepare the evening's dinner.

"Okay, come a little closer. We've loaded one last tray and you can snag one."

"I totally came in here to snag." And escape. Everywhere she looked she made eye contact with Bryce. It seemed impossible not to notice him.

When she wasn't caught in Bryce's gaze, Drew kept her attention with sweet words and interesting thoughts, but there was no zing of attraction. No uncontrollable awareness that made her crave to be touched and check one night stand off the list. Same with Aiden, who'd whispered in her ear that he'd love to see her later tonight.

She picked up a taco, took a big bite, and moaned as it made its way down to her stomach. "I want to marry this taco."

"Lucky taco."

Honor stilled. That voice. That one-of-a-kind masculine scent. Bryce stood right behind her. She put the rest of the taco in her mouth, chewed without sound effects and turned. "Have you tried one?" She snagged one more before Elena's assistant picked up the tray. "Here." Her fingers grazed his lips as she held the taco to his mouth and he took a bite.

Big mistake.

He watched her watch him, the connection making her hot. She pushed the rest of the taco in and pulled her arm back. He caught her wrist and brought her hand back up toward his mouth. Eating had never been so sexy before. Well, except for the other day when he'd eaten the fritter and she'd wanted to lick him. The way his throat moved, holy three alarm fire. She wished she had another taco to give him.

The sips of champagne, romantic atmosphere, and stolen glances were obviously working against their restraint because neither of them seemed overly concerned with the electricity crackling between them. The intense feelings that had overcome her the night they'd met and that she couldn't extinguish no matter how often she told herself it was wrong, were back in full force.

He chewed and swallowed and then with a very slow, deliberate motion, he licked her index finger, then her middle finger. Any coherent thoughts she had spiraled into the abyss. She had no idea the tips of her fingers could send a rush of pleasure between her thighs. When his lips wrapped around her thumb her legs shook and she moaned an entirely different kind of murmur than the one a few moments ago.

"I see the attraction," he said, his voice husky.

"It's hard to deny."

"It's hard all right."

Honor snapped her eyes shut and pulled her hand back. "This is not okay," she said, hoping to extinguish the flirtatious flames raising her body temperature. She brushed by him in a rush to get out of the kitchen and put some much needed distance between them.

He grabbed her hand and tugged her through the sliding glass door that led outside. "We need to talk," he said.

"No, we don't." Her bare feet happily met the sand, though, the cold, soft grains between her toes cooling everything warm inside her.

He shot her a heated look that erased the whole cooling thing. "Fine by me. We'll talk after."

"After what exactly?" Because being alone with the guy

she couldn't get out of her head on a beach under the stars meant one thing. Kissing. Touching.

Or so her renegade body hoped.

"That's up to you." He plowed through the sand like it didn't take any extra effort.

"Me? You're the one dragging me out here like he's about to go off." She would not admit she felt the same way.

"You're right." He came to an abrupt stop, wrapped his arm around her waist, and brought her flush against him. "I can't think straight when I'm near you."

Neither could she. Pressed against his solid chest, his muscled thighs, and the hardness in between, the only thing on her mind was getting skin to skin. The sounds of the wedding party were somewhere behind them, the ocean lapped leisurely at the shoreline. In their secluded spot in the sand, nothing seemed to exist but the two of them.

"I have that affect on people," she said.

"Yeah? And what do you do about it?"

All she had to do was lift up on her tiptoes and her lips could touch his, but there was only one move to make if she had any hope of salvaging her resistance to him. "Let me show you."

She squeezed a hand between their bodies and pushed him in the chest to knock him off balance. Caught unaware, he wavered before shifting with a step back, eyebrows arched in surprise. She put all her weight on her left leg, smiled, then used her right foot to sweep Bryce's foot out from under him at the same time she lifted and pulled him by the shirt. A split second later, he had no choice but to go down when she let go of his shirt.

Only he grabbed her by the arms and in a surprise move, brought her down too, cushioning her fall with his.

"Hey! Let go of me."

He rolled her right over, covered her body with his. "Judo

Foot Sweep. Nice."

Honor blew a strand of hair away from her mouth. He had her pinned in the sand, and she didn't like it. Mostly. She wiggled in hopes of jostling him off, but he barely moved. "My dress is getting ruined."

"Is that really what you're worried about?" He settled on his elbows, his warm breath tickled the side of her neck.

"Yes."

"I don't think so."

Crap on a cracker. Did he have to feel so good and look so good and know how to read her? "I thought we established you have a thinking problem."

He laughed. The rumble through his chest reverberated through hers. She smiled despite the effort to keep her lips pressed together in a straight line.

"I need to kiss you, Honor. One kiss the way I want to kiss you, and then we can be done."

She closed her eyes thinking maybe when she opened them he'd be gone and she'd discover she'd hit her head on her way to the kitchen and dreamed the last ten minutes.

Nope. Not a dream.

"Tell me what you want." He shifted his hips, leaving no doubt as to how much he desired her.

But it wasn't just that. It was the way he looked at her, with hunger yes, but also something more. His gaze took her away from everything but the two of them.

She didn't deserve attention from a guy like Bryce, but right here, right now, she'd be a fool not to take what he offered. Just this once.

"I want you to kiss me." More than she'd ever wanted anything. She prayed the painful admission didn't hurt her quiet talks with Payton.

His smile, a little mischievous around the edges, had her melting into the sand. Then his lips brushed hers, and the stars collided. She cupped his face in her hands and shut her eyes.

Kissing had always ranked high on her list of favorite things to do, but Bryce took it to a whole new level. Forget about his mouth on her fingertips, *this* linked to all her happy zones and more.

He'd literally swept her off her feet and his kiss quickened the beat of her heart. His lips were soft and warm and hungry. His kiss moved through her like warm honey, filling all the places inside her that had been cold for so long.

He slid his tongue along the seam of her lips, licking her before he pressed further. She willingly opened to him, stroked his tongue, kissed him harder. He groaned. He tasted like champagne and everything good as he delved deeper and committed a full-on assault inside her mouth. His hand gripped her waist. They sank further into the sand.

She clutched his shoulders, smoothed her palms down his back. He pulled gruffly away, nipped at her ear. "You have no idea how much I want you," he said.

"Tell me," she murmured. She slipped her hands lower, covered his very fine butt, and ground her pelvis against him.

"I want to lift this dress and do you right here."

His gravelly voice combined with the thick, hard length pressing into her stomach made her almost breathless. He kissed her jaw, her neck. His warm breath fanned over her collarbone before he lifted and fused his mouth to hers once again.

The kiss rammed every objection out of her bliss-hazed mind. With her fingers in his hair, she kissed him back. He caressed her mouth with perfect care and passion one minute and hot, out of control lashes the next. The hand at her waist moved up to her breast. He cupped it, rubbed his thumb over her nipple. She spiraled close to the edge of release, just like she had the first night they'd met, when his barely R-rated touch set her body aflame with more feeling than she'd ever thought possible.

"Bryce," she whispered against his lips.

"Okay," he relented, as if knew he'd pushed her to the edge and she needed him to stop. He rolled to the side and helped her sit up, wiping her back of sand.

She pressed her fingers to her well-kissed lips, wanting to feel a little longer this incredible moment in the sand.

He jammed his fingers through his hair. "I'm sorry. I shouldn't have gotten so carried away."

All the feel-good sensations making her forget her loneliness fled. The regret in his voice pierced through her skin and bones. She wasn't sorry. What kind of person did that make her?

They stared toward the water in silence.

"What did you want to talk about?" Honor asked, not sure talking was any better than kissing, but the quiet bothered her. She didn't want to end things tonight on a bad note.

"Payton's list."

Would everything with Bryce come back to Payton? Her heart went on lockdown. "No, thanks."

"I can't pretend I didn't see it."

"Yes, you can." She glanced at his profile. "Why does it even matter to you?" She knew the answer to that, didn't she? Payton still mattered to him and he wanted to know more about her best friend. Make sense of a list that maybe surprised him? Payton hadn't been the easiest person to get to know. There were days even Honor felt like she was pulling teeth to get her friend to talk.

"I thought I knew the girl I was falling for, but now I'm second guessing everything we had," he said in a quiet voice. "Payton broke my heart and I guess a part of me is still trying to figure out why." He wiped at some sand on his pant leg.

"I don't know what to tell you," Honor whispered. She hadn't agreed with Payton's decision to cut Bryce out of her life, but the choice hadn't belonged to her.

He cast her a quick glance. "I've been thinking. Helping people is my business. It's what I do know. My clients have lists. Things they want to accomplish. And I help them achieve their goals. Helping you with Payton's list would help me, too. It's my chance to say good-bye."

Honor choked back tears. Whether she liked it or not, she and Bryce had Payton in common and running away from him wouldn't change that.

For several minutes they stared out to the inky, calm sea in quiet solidarity before Bryce broke the silence with, "There's a place to hot air balloon not far from here."

"Escondido. I know. That was the first thing I crossed off the list."

"How was it?" he asked with genuine interest.

Honor sighed and wrapped her arms around her knees. "Amazing."

"Payton wanted to experience a birds-eye view?"

"We both did. She was afraid of heights. Even the thought of standing on a ladder freaked her out. But ever since we'd watched the movie Casanova with the scene of a hot air balloon ride over Venice, and I'd told her how much I wanted to try it, she wanted to work up the courage to try it, too."

"Good thing you don't share her same fear."

"We were actually really different. I think that's why we made such good friends. We complemented each other."

She'd never talked about Payton like this with anyone else before and it was nice. After Pay passed away a general sadness fell over the town and by quiet agreement her memory stayed mostly in people's minds. Payton's parents moved to San Francisco to be closer to their son and his wife and life went on in their small beach community.

Bryce angled his foot so it touched hers. "Do you have a tattoo I can try and find?"

Knowing Bryce wanted to search her body for a tattoo put all sorts of dirty thoughts in her mind that should not be there. "Not yet."

"Not yet as in it's too soon for me to look? Or not yet you don't have one?"

She worked really hard not to smile. "I don't have one."

He raised his eyebrows in question. She jumped to her feet. "We'd better get back to the party." He'd already gotten her to say too much. Think and feel too much.

He put a hand on her arm to slow her speed walk. "What's the deal?"

"No deal. Just done talking about the list. And I'd like to remind you to keep quiet about it. This is only between us." She gave him a side-glance.

"I'm not going to tell anyone, but come on. Why haven't you gotten a tattoo yet? That's the easiest thing on there."

"None of your business." Did the guy ever stop with the questions? He should've been a lawyer rather than an agent.

He brought her to a halt by gently gripping her arm before sliding his fingers down to grasp her hand. "Come on. We've come this far. Don't hold out on me now."

His amiable tone combined with *that* face was totally unfair. She hated the power he had over her. Hated that one look at him turned her into Chatty Cathy.

"I'm afraid of needles," she relented. Her shoulders sagged.

"That's a common fear," he said without judgment. "Did something happen to trigger it?"

He stared at her and waited for more. Damn those irresistible eyes.

"When I was nine I had to give blood for some reason I can't remember. The nurse couldn't get my vein the first time so someone else came in. That person was worse. She had trouble too, and then panicked when I squirmed and she hit a nerve in my arm. I remember the pain shooting to my fingertips and I screamed. Ever since then I've been afraid of needles."

He brought her hand up to his mouth and kissed her knuckles. "Getting a tattoo is a lot different than giving blood."

She admired his mouth and how it made everything better. "I know. But just the thought of it makes me sweat. I'd be mortified if I passed out while getting it done."

"Have you passed out before?"

"No, but I always have to lie down for shots and my heart races and I can't look and it's really nerve racking."

"I could go with you." He dropped her arm and started to walk.

The bright, festive lights at Zane and Sophie's house lit up the beach. Voices muffled a minute ago grew clearer. That's where she needed to be. Surrounded by people and noise and more champagne. She needed distance before she drowned in Bryce's attention. Plenty of guys were nice to her. But none had made her feel this way. And none had ever shared a secret this big with her before. So even though she wanted to toss his suggestion into the ocean where the fish could chew on it, she had to entertain his offer.

"Honor?"

"Maybe."

"Fair enough."

She forced a smile. There was absolutely nothing fair about the way her emotions had hijacked her rules for relationships. And her loyalty to her best friend.

"I never would have guessed Payton wanted a tattoo," he added, the tease and warmth in his voice disappearing.

"I know. It is out of character for her, but she did keep some things private."

"Even from you?"

"Even from me."

. . .

Bryce slipped off his sunglasses and walked into the Happy Harpoon. No one stood at the check-in desk, but Midge passed by running her hands down her *Happy* apron.

"Hey there, handsome. Grab a seat anywhere you like."

Bryce nodded at the silver-haired whirlwind and found a small booth that afforded him a view of the entrance. With time to spare before his lunch meeting with Cooper, he pulled out his cell to call Danny back and let him know no worries on not making it, but his phone chimed with a text message first.

*Hey son, sorry it took me a few days to get back to you. Congrats on the new client. Proud of you.*

*Thanks, Dad. About to have lunch with my next new client, I hope.*

*The skateboarder?*

*Cooper Mitchell. Kid's got it and I want it.* Bryce looked up and said, "thanks" to the waitress for dropping off a menu.

*I've no doubt you'll get him then. Dinner soon?*

*Yeah. Tell Mom I said hi.*

*Call - don't text - her and tell her yourself.*

Bryce chuckled as he sat back and thought about his dad. As one of the best defense attorneys in Los Angeles, James Bishop played it heartless in the courtroom. But with Bryce and his younger sister the old guy was all heart. He pushed, sure, but only to the point he knew his kids could handle it. Bryce owed his strength of purpose to his dad.

"Bishop, you hanging around our town on a daily basis now?"

Blinking away his thoughts, Bryce focused on the ex-football player towering over the table. "Hey, Tango. Yeah, I've got a meeting with Cooper Mitchell."

Tango nodded. "I'm thinking of making a comeback. Think you could handle me?"

Bryce chuckled. "As soon as they start the senior league, I'll let you know."

"Boy, I am never gonna be a senior and you'd best remember that." He flexed his biceps, the muscles bulging underneath his short sleeves. Point taken. The guy could probably lift a truck over his head.

"You showing off for me, old man? Because I should tell you, it's working."

Tango threw his head back and laughed. "Too bad my lady friend looks to be getting impatient." Bryce followed Tango's line of sight to see a woman waving her hand. "I'm sure I could teach you a few things," Tango added, eyebrows raised, before he moved on. Cooper took the seat across from Bryce two seconds later.

"Hey, Mr. Bishop. Sorry I'm a minute late."

Bryce took note of Coop's slight but safe rebellious look. No doubt he'd appeal to both guys and girls and bring a whole new set of fans to skateboarding. The good-looking gene definitely ran in the Mitchell family. "No worries. And call me Bryce. Mr. Bishop is my dad."

Cooper blinked like he wasn't sure he wanted to be that friendly. "Mind if I say something first?"

"Not at all."

"I noticed something between you and my sister at the wedding and I want to remind you that my skateboarding and my family don't mix."

Bryce stiffened. He'd thought about Sunday night countless times. When he and Honor had fallen into the sand after the wedding and he'd finally gotten to lick inside her mouth, he *had* almost gone off. Then to talk like they had about Payton's list, he knew getting closer was the wrong way to go if he wanted Coop as a client. He and Danny had worked too hard to restore their reputation for Bryce to blow it now.

But sometimes lines blurred. Made more muddy by a shared past with Honor he couldn't ignore if he wanted to move forward.

"I hear you," Bryce said. "Your sister and I were just being friendly. I dated Payton before she passed away."

"You were the guy she snuck off to see?"

"Yeah." He'd never understood why she wanted to keep their relationship a secret and had been glad when she'd finally talked about bringing him to White Strand.

"You never came around when she was sick."

"She broke things off before I knew."

Cooper gave a small nod. "She pretty much broke things off with everyone except my sister."

Huh. He hadn't imagined Payton tuning out everyone. He leaned forward with his elbows on the table. "So you're ready to go pro," he said, steering the conversation to a much safer topic.

Coop's expression went from guarded to psyched. "I am," he said around a smile.

The waitress stopped at their table with another menu. Coop waved it off saying he knew what he wanted. They ordered, talked about the skateboarding world and what Bryce would do for Cooper and his career. An hour flew by in easy camaraderie.

Bryce knew the kid needed time to think about things.

Knew that Jake Harrington, one of the best sports agents out there, and Bryce's adversary on more than one occasion, wanted Cooper. But he offered representation anyway and said he'd wait for as long as it took for a decision. It wasn't something he normally did, but Coop had Bryce's gut clenching. Beyond skateboarding, Bryce sensed the kid had more of a story to share in the years to come. Coop's abilities would undoubtedly improve, but his optimism after suffering an almost life altering accident earned him a special distinction.

Coop's cell buzzed with a text message. "Sorry, man. It's from my sister." He read the small screen and rolled his eyes with brotherly love. "She's got a problem."

"She okay?" Bryce asked.

"It's work." Coop's fingers flew over the screen to text back a message.

"The antique shop?" Bryce waved to the waitress and mouthed, "Check."

"No. It's this Valentine's Day thing she's in charge of for the mayor's office. Her antique store is a total afterthought."

Bryce frowned. He didn't think that true. "She seemed pretty stoked about it to me."

Coop lifted his head and studied Bryce with watchful intensity. "Maybe she'll keep working on it and buying things to sell, but she'll probably never open it."

"Why not?"

"She's worried about it failing." Panic creased his forehead. "I shouldn't have told you that. She'd have my balls if she found out."

"How does she know it will fail unless she tries?" Bryce took the check from the waitress and pulled out his wallet.

"That's just it. She doesn't follow through on stuff. She's got a really short attention span." He pressed his lips together. "Shouldn't have said that either."

But it's on Payton's list, Bryce thought. He had no idea what things Honor might have tried in the past, but he'd stake everything that this time it mattered.

"Thanks for lunch," Coop said, easing out of the booth. "I'll be in touch." His phone buzzed again. He looked at it, let out an unhappy breath and texted something. "I hate this," he muttered, pocketing his phone.

Bryce followed him outside. "Is there something I can do to help?" The offer flew out of his mouth before he could stop it.

"This was a good meeting, Mr. Bishop. But like I told you, my family, especially my sister, isn't any of your concern."

"I'm clear on that," Bryce said. "I have a little time to kill and thought if I could help *you* out, I would." Truth. After bonding the last hour with Cooper, he'd do anything to get on his good side and up his chances of getting him as a client.

"You know how to get a hundred and fifty pairs of roller skates by tomorrow?"

"Honor needs skates?"

They reached the sidewalk and stopped. Blue colored the sky, but scattered clouds played hide and seek with the sun. The cool breeze carried the scent of salty, fresh air.

"You know how they have Walk to School day? She came up with this idea to skate to work on Valentine's Day. The mayor's been trying to implement some healthy heart, wellness program without much success, I guess, so Honor thought it would be fun to"—he put his hands up and made air quotes—"'Roll Into Work.' All the city workplaces like the mayor's office, fire and police station, library, local paper, are on board. Honor rented skates for them. Only they weren't delivered today as promised. She's freaking out and wanted me to help her figure something out."

Bryce tried to picture Honor losing her patience and couldn't see it. She'd be fired up, yeah, but she wouldn't want anyone to notice this minor setback. That must be why she called her brother.

"I actually do know someone who could probably get her the skates."

"Dude, seriously? That would be killer." He shifted his weight and glanced at the sidewalk. "Would you mind going over to her office? I've got to be somewhere in five minutes."

"Not a problem. She's at City Hall?"

"Yeah."

They shook hands, Cooper's grip tighter than necessary. Bryce understood. Honor was off limits. He reminded himself of that over and over again as he headed down Main Street on foot. He'd been to City Hall once before during the film festival last summer and it wasn't far.

He pushed through the double doors of the small building and stopped at the reception desk. The older woman grinned up at him. A badge on her shirt said Shirley. He smiled, remembering Honor's mention of the woman.

"Hello," Shirley said. "Can I help you?"

"How are you today, Shirley?"

"I'm well, thank you."

"That's a very nice blue streak. It goes with your blouse."

Her smile widened, pink spread across her cheeks, and she patted the strip of blue in her short, straight brown hair. "Thank you. My granddaughter did it for me."

"I'm here to see Honor Mitchell. Can you point me in the right direction?"

"She's just down the hall there. Last office on the right." Shirley motioned over her shoulder. "Can I ask what your business is with her?"

Bryce admired the sweet concern in Shirley's voice, but he didn't think Honor would want him sharing. "Is it required before I pass go?"

Shirley's posture slouched. "No."

"How about we call it a friendly matter then," he leaned his elbows on the desk, "and keep it between you and me?"

She grinned. He winked.

Black and white pictures of White Strand dating back decades lined the hallway as he passed several offices until he reached a small corner room not much bigger than the closet he had played kissing games with Honor in. One small wooden chair with a pale yellow seat cushion and a tall but thin bookshelf took up what little empty space remained. A painting of sunflowers hung on the wall. The pen atop her desk had a plastic pink flower attached to the end of it.

He knocked on the open door.

Honor looked up from the mess of papers on her tiny desk. Her pretty blue-gray eyes widened when she saw him. "Bryce?"

"Hi. I was having lunch with your brother and he told me what happened. We think I might be able to help." He purposely said 'we' to keep her defenses down.

"With my brother," she muttered, as if she didn't like the two of them meeting. She dropped her head into her hand and rubbed her forehead. "Close the door?"

"Sure." Once shut, he leaned against it.

"This is what I get for not following up before today. The rental company says they never got my order and there's no way they can pull together over a hundred pairs of skates and have them here by tomorrow. I thought Coop might know someone he could call to help."

Bryce stepped away from the door. "A friend of mine owns a skate shop in L.A. He's the guy TV and film people go to when they need huge quantities of skates or boards. You need one-fifty?"

Honor blinked and nodded.

He pulled out his cell and made the call. His buddy got on the line and a minute later Bryce said, "Where do you want them delivered?"

Honor's gorgeous lips parted, but no sound came out. She took a deep breath. The white sweater with rhinestone buttons clung to her perfectly round breasts, and he ran a hand down his pant leg to stop the itch in the tips of his fingers.

"Here," she finally said and rattled off the address.

Just as he said goodbye, she jumped to her feet. "Wait. What's the rental fee? When do they need payment? What about sizes? How long is the rental for?"

The cell phone on her desk rang. "It's Coop." She picked it up. "Hey," she said with a raised voice before she pressed something on the screen and put the phone down. "I've got you on speaker."

"Is Bryce there?"

"He's here and just saved my ass."

"Awesome. Thanks, bro. No way could I have pulled anything off this fast."

"My pleasure."

"H, you good then?"

"Always," she said, rather unconvincingly to Bryce's ears.

"Okay. See ya later."

The second Coop clicked off, the air in the room changed, like time had slowed to keep him and Honor together for as long as they wanted. He sat in the chair and met her soft yet vivid gaze.

"I don't know what to say," she murmured.

"I was happy to help. And to answer your questions, the rental fee is taken care of, they know what sizes to send, and if you could return them by Monday, that would be great. They'll be here in the morning, by the way."

"What do you mean the rental fee is taken care of?"

"It's a donation. It's heart month, right?"

She rubbed the side of her neck. "No. I mean yes, but we can't accept that. That's... that's..."

He stood, walked around her desk, and squeezed in behind her chair. "That's how it is. So how about a, 'Thank you, Bryce, I owe you one,' and we'll call it even." He wrapped his hands around her shoulders and started to massage. He'd been told, "I don't need you to rescue me," by a few ex-girlfriends, but he couldn't change who he was. And maybe that was part of his problem. Maybe that's what had kept Payton away. Maybe he knew his actions would ultimately push Honor away and that's what got his feet to move behind her chair. He wanted to be close to her for as long as it lasted.

"What are you—"

"Shh. Just relax and let me work the tension out of your neck."

Her chin dropped. "Owing you isn't even."

"Figured that out, did you? Well, I need a favor, too." Through the thin material of her sweater the muscles under his fingers stiffened but he was helpless to stop the request on the tip of his tongue. "I want to pick your brain about Roseville pottery."

She lifted her head. "You're not going to let it go, are you?"

"Let it—?" She meant the list. "I'm serious about the Roseville, nothing else. My mom is a big collector and her birthday is next month. I'd like to hire you to help me find a piece to give to her."

Honor peeked over her shoulder at him. "Hire me?"

"You're an antique dealer, aren't you?"

Her eyes alighted with pleasure before she turned away and dropped her head again. His chest filled with a kind of contented energy he'd never felt before.

"Okay," she whispered.

It took everything he had not to kiss her nape, move up to her earlobe, then around to her smooth cheek, her lush lips. Eye on the prize, dude. And it isn't Honor.

"Does Saturday work for you?" he asked.

"Sure."

He continued to massage her shoulders and neck until her body melted under his touch and she let out a hum that had the strain against his zipper jumping up a few degrees. If he didn't walk out the door right now, he'd stop at nothing short of sitting her on her desk, lifting her skirt, and burying his face between her legs.

Not the tactic to win over her brother and put his agency back at the top of its game.

# Chapter Six

Honor's body had never betrayed her like this before. She couldn't stop thinking about lying in the sand with Bryce. His mouth on hers. And when she did that, thoughts of having those sexy lips of his kiss every inch of her skin consumed her.

That he also used said mouth to say nice things and help her at work caused her to suffer a constant state of arousal since he'd left her office two days ago. She glanced down. Yep, her nipples were hard and poking through her sweater. She needed a bra with armor stat.

And her sense of rightness checked. She hadn't uttered a single thought to Payton in days. Sweet plus sexy could not equal Bryce.

"How do I stop on these things?" Shirley yelled, skating past the park bench Honor sat on in the middle of town.

Honor fanned her sweater away from her chest. "Skate onto the grass," she called. Shirley gave a thumbs-up as she coasted to a halt.

Roll Into Work had been a huge success so far. Skaters had overtaken the bike lanes and sidewalks this morning, young and old alike taking part whether they had a workplace to go to or not. Honor had stopped at the supermarket to pick up bran muffins and fresh fruit for the mayor's office, and several employees had left their skates on, skating around the aisles like they were in a grocery store derby and laughing the whole time.

Shirley plopped down beside her. "I think I pulled a muscle."

"Ouch. Really?" Honor winced. "Would it help if I told you, you looked great skating?"

"Enough about me." Shirley tapped her arm. "Tell me about the hot stuff that came in to see you the other day."

"Hot stu—you mean Bryce?"

"So that's his name."

Crap. She'd just told TMZ's most faithful watcher way too much. The clock on the bell tower chimed, drawing Honor's eye to the time and the clear sky above. An airplane flew silently in the distance. Maybe by ring twelve Shirley would lose interest.

Or pull a tongue muscle so she couldn't talk.

She did not just think that. Bad Honor. Was it even possible to injure your tongue like that?

Maybe with Bryce—oh my god, she had to stop thinking about him like that. "Shouldn't you be manning the front desk?" Honor asked sweetly.

"I'm on my lunch break. Are you two dating?"

Honor bit back a groan. Shirley and her band of gossip girls disguised as sweet little old ladies had known Honor her whole life. They meant well, but they wanted every young person married off. "No."

"Why not?"

Honor pressed two fingers to her temple. "It's complicated."

Shirley put her hand on Honor's knee. "He has a

girlfriend?"

No, but… "Something like that." Not for the first time she wondered if giving in to her desires meant betraying Payton. Her best friend was gone. She and Bryce clicked. But even so, she couldn't trust herself not to disappoint him somehow. Or do something to hurt him. And that thought bothered her more than having something that was once Pay's.

"Hey, H., Mrs. B.," Cooper said. Honor had never been happier to see her brother.

"Hello, Cooper," Shirley said.

"Mind if I talk to my sister?"

Shirley frowned, obviously not done with her interrogation. Honor smiled at her as she stood. "Of course."

Coop took Shirley's spot and the two of them watched her skate away. "Looked like you wanted to crawl out of your skin there."

"Thanks for the rescue."

"Always. Hey, I'm heading to LA now and I'll be back sometime tomorrow night. I'm crashing at Ty's house."

"You're meeting with that other agent?" She posed it as a question, but she knew the answer.

"Don't sound so happy about it."

"I'm not." She turned to face him more squarely. "Are you sure—"

"Chill or I'm not going to say anything more about it to you." He drilled her with blue eyes that seemed far more mature than his nineteen years. "I'm an adult. I can make my own decisions."

"Whatever." She crossed her arms and slouched back against the bench. He might think he knew best, but he didn't. Not that Honor did, but as the older sibling she should.

"Honor?"

She looked up and found Aiden blocking the sun. "Hi, Aiden." She sat up taller.

"I thought that was you." Aiden turned to Coop. "And it's Cooper, right? We met at Zane's wedding."

"Yo," her brother said, taking in Aiden like he had very sharp devil horns poking out of his sun-bleached hair.

"I wasn't sure if you were still in town," Honor said.

"I'm leaving tomorrow." His nice green eyes shouted player and they were on her like crazy glue.

Hmm. Leaving tomorrow. Cute. Nice. Interested. Could she tick off her one night stand with him? With all these insane thoughts about Bryce she really needed to let off some sexual steam. She got to her feet. "Where are you headed?"

"Hawaii." His gaze took a nice slow stroll down her body.

Cooper jumped up. "H, a word?" He linked his arm with hers and tugged.

"Excuse me a minute," she said over her shoulder, then to Coop, "What are you doing?"

He took several more steps before stopping. "The guy wants in your pants."

"I know."

"And you're okay with that? What is wrong with you?"

"You know what? You don't want me in your business, so keep out of mine."

Irritation rolled off Coop's puffed out chest. "Personal business is different. I'm not gonna let this guy take advantage of you."

Honor bristled at his choice of words. She could damn well take care of herself. "No one is taking advantage of me. I'm a big girl."

"I know something happened at Dad's company party and you won't talk about it, but ever since then you've been totally closed off. This dude does not deserve whatever you want to give him." Coop slanted his head so he spoke into her ear. "I saw him leave the Harpoon with a girl two nights ago, H, don't add to his scorecard."

Her brother didn't get it. Aiden was the perfect one night stand. She needed a guy she didn't feel anything for so she could cross the deed off Payton's list without worry of getting attached.

But the thought of him with another girl just the other night didn't sit right. There was also the chance she'd see him again since he and Zane were friends.

She spun around and stepped toward Aiden. "Sorry about that."

"No problem." He smiled. "You busy later? I can't think of anyone prettier to spend dinner with before I go."

Sweet talker. Say yes. *Say you'd love to. Coop will be gone. You can bring Aiden home with you.* "I am actually. But thanks for asking." Stupid principles.

"My loss. It was nice meeting you."

"You, too."

Aiden lifted his chin to Coop and took off. "I knew you couldn't do it," Coop said, his hand landing on her shoulder.

She shrugged off his touch. She damn well could do it and she'd prove it. As soon as she met the perfect stranger. "I could have. I just needed to set a good example."

Coop laughed. "Yeah, you tell yourself that." He took in her scowl. "Hey, for real, though, you're the best sister a guy could have." He wrapped her in a hug. "That's why I stick my nose where it doesn't belong."

"Right back at you," she said, squeezing him tight. One good thing that had come out his accident was they'd grown much closer. And she'd never do anything to ruin that bond.

At seven o'clock that night, Honor curled up on her couch and scrolled through Netflix. She had a date with *Breakfast at Tiffany's*.

"You with me, Pay? It's time for some Audrey Hepburn. I remember when you dressed as her for Halloween. God, you looked exactly like her."

Just as the opening scene popped onto her TV screen the doorbell rang. Perfect timing. She paused the movie, grabbed the twenty on the ottoman, and padded to the door in her socks.

Only it wasn't the usual Japanese food delivery guy standing on her porch. "Bryce?"

"Hi, Honor." He lifted the take-out bag. "I know this probably looks like I'm a creeper or something, but I'm really not. I happened to be at the restaurant picking up my own food when I heard the name 'Honor.' The delivery guy was running behind so I offered to swing by and drop it off. Here you go." He handed her the bag. "That'll be sixteen seventy-eight."

His grin flashed like a hundred shooting stars, and wishes about kissing him again filled her head. The smile also stole her voice. She handed him the twenty.

He didn't take it. "I'm kidding. It's on me."

She continued to stare at him like a mute madwoman. Bryce stood at her door in jeans and a tan button down, loose at the collar, the skin at this neck soft and—she leaned a little bit closer—smelling deliciously male. His hair was messier than normal and she wanted to run her fingers through it.

"Okay, well, have a good night." He started to back away.

"Wait." What was wrong with her? She never had trouble talking to guys. "You just happened to be here? That does sound kind of creepy," she teased, secretly happy to see him again.

He stopped his steps. A small smile lifted the corners of his mouth. "Zane called. He asked if I'd swing by his house to make sure the surprise he got for Sophie arrived okay."

"Did it?" She wanted to ask what surprise, but held back.

Sophie would no doubt want to share the news.

"Yes."

"Do you want to come in and eat?" What was she doing? Her mouth had decided to operate on its own free will. "I mean I'm guessing you were going to eat on your drive home and that's not really safe."

"Thanks, but I should..." His brows furrowed in concentration, or maybe it was debate. Whatever it was, several seconds of silence only magnified the charged air particles between them.

"It's okay," she said. "Thanks for the special delivery." She leaned on the door to close it.

"Hold on. I'd like to come in." He ran to his car and grabbed his own brown bag.

Super happy for his company, she swung the door wide as he approached. His arm brushed hers when he stepped inside and the contact, combined with how good he smelled, had her a little weak in the knees.

"Table? Couch?" He asked, looking like he belonged in her house.

"Couch. I was about to watch a movie." She hurried into the kitchen to grab forks, napkins and another bottle of water.

"Is Cooper here?"

"No. He's in LA to... " Was Bryce really here hoping to talk to her brother?

"To meet with another agent?"

"Yes." She leaned against the kitchen counter for a moment to stop the sudden shake in her legs.

"You okay?" Bryce asked.

She turned to find him right beside her. He picked the napkins and forks up off the counter. "Do you honestly think he's ready to go pro?"

"I do."

"What if I don't?"

Bryce didn't just look at her, he seemed to look inside her with genuine regard. "I get that you're worried about him, but that isn't a good reason to keep him from following his dreams."

"You don't know—"

"I know more than you think." He twisted around and walked back to the couch, leaving her to dwell on what he meant.

He sat in the middle of her sofa, leaving just enough room for her on either side. Her stomach fluttered at the idea that even though they might not agree on Cooper, he wanted to be close to her. When she sat and her bare knee touched his covered one, the quivers intensified. And, oh crap. She looked down at herself. She'd forgotten she only had on her Victoria's Secret sleep shirt.

She haphazardly dropped the bottles of water onto the ottoman. "I'm going to put on some sweats."

Bryce took hold of her arm. "You don't need to change on my account."

What about on her account? She needed more of a barrier between her nakedness and his nearness because she definitely wasn't thinking about food or Tiffany's. She was thinking about straddling his lap and licking his neck.

And she didn't think she'd imagined the predatory gleam in his eyes. He might be as conflicted as her about what they were doing, but the attraction couldn't be refuted.

If he wasn't going to let her bareness bother him, though, then she wouldn't let it bother her either. "Okay," she relented.

"What movie are we watching?" He opened the Styrofoam lid on his take-out.

She tucked one leg under her bottom and got busy with her own food. "*Breakfast at Tiffany's*. It's one of my favorites."

He made a face, no doubt wishing he'd scored an action film instead, but lifted the remote and pressed play. She stifled a giggle. And swallowed a shiver when he gave her a sidelong glance that tracked from her face down to her legs before he took a bite of his dinner.

Somehow halfway through the movie, Honor found herself nestled next to him. His arm was wrapped around her, her head and hand were on his chest, and rather than hear the words coming from the characters on the TV, she heard the beating of his heart. Felt each *lub-dub* like a song she wanted to play on repeat over and over and over again. She thought about the quote she remembered best from the movie...

*"You know what's wrong with you, Miss Whoever-You-Are? You're chicken. You've got no guts. You're afraid to stick out your chin and say, 'Okay, life's a fact, people do fall in love, people do belong to each other, because that's the only chance anybody's got for real happiness.'"*

Honor had never thought herself a chicken, only matter-of-fact. She couldn't change her feathers.

But was it true? If she never took another chance on love, would she ever be truly happy? Part of her wanted what Sophie and Zane had.

The other part made it her mission to fly free.

With a gentle touch, Bryce tickled the hand she had on his chest with the tips of his fingers. Lazy strokes across her knuckles, her skin. "I feel you thinking," he whispered. "You okay?"

No she was not okay. She was in trouble. Big, big trouble. Not only did he always seem in tune to her, he made her think about things she'd written off. This crazy reaction to him was different from anything she's experienced before.

"Yes," she half lied. Because being in his arms felt amazing and she didn't want to move from this position.

His tickling stopped and he put one of the small couch pillows in his lap. He shifted his weight, keeping one arm wrapped around her shoulder, until her head fell onto the pillow. Then his fingers gently rubbed up and down her arm, her back. Her eyes fluttered shut.

"How'd the skating go today?"

"Good. Everyone seemed to really like it. And as far as I know there weren't any casualties. The mayor also told me I was da bomb, so you know, I think that means he'll be giving me a key to the city soon."

"You know what that means, right?" His fingers dipped a little below her lower back, teasing the top of her bottom before cruising up her side.

"That I can't hide it in a rock?"

He chuckled. She smiled. "That congratulations are in order. I think you're the first person to successfully bring roller-skating back."

"Thanks to you."

"I'm pretty sure you did it without me." His hand rubbed farther down, this time rounding the curve of her butt. Her nightshirt rose a little up her legs when his palm massaged back up to her shoulder.

Her eyes flew open. Tingles of anticipation shot straight to between her thighs. What was he doing? And please, Lord, don't let him stop.

She swallowed and concentrated on the movie. She also didn't move a muscle.

He accepted her silence by continuing to rub her back before moving his ministrations to her hip and dipping his hand to her front, the pads of his fingers grazing the side of her stomach and front of her thigh before pressing lightly back up her torso.

With each stroke down her body, he got more daring, more intimate. Her shirt inched up higher, exposing her black cheeky panties. He let out a tiny groan when he touched the lace that only covered half her bottom.

That barely-there sexy sound almost had her lifting her

head to see if he was as turned on as she was, but she didn't want to spoil the best back rub of her life. Every sweep of his hand up and down made her belly coil tighter in pleasure, her skin more sensitive.

She almost stopped breathing when he lifted her shirt high enough to expose her entire backside. His warm, strong hand settled at the base of her spine and stilled. Was he silently asking permission to continue? Staring at her ass and contemplating his next move?

*Touch me* there. "There" being that magical spot that ached and begged to have a turn with at least two of his fingers. She rolled her hips over just the tiniest bit. Spread her legs just the slightest bit. But otherwise kept her hands around the pillow in his lap and her head still, eyes on the television screen.

He slipped his hand over the curve of her waist and to the edge of her panties. She rotated a little more, lest he doubt where she wanted him to go.

Her breath came out in a short sigh the second he rubbed over her center. She didn't feel the least bit shameful as her legs fell open and she pressed into his hand. Her heels dug into the couch, she squeezed the pillow.

"Mmm," escaped her lips. He continued to massage, his thumb grazing over her tight nub and making her crazy. Wet. Horny beyond horny. He slipped his hand underneath the cotton and lace and the feel of his bare hand was almost more than she could take.

Until he slid one, then two fingers inside her.

She cried out and came faster and harder than she could ever remember.

He brought her down slowly, caressing with such delicate strokes that she was afraid to look at him. Afraid to speak. Raw, complicated feelings she had no idea how to handle opened her mind to a new sensation—trust.

Bryce covered her back up with her shirt and rested his hand on her upper arm. He settled deeper into the couch as if he were content to end this there. She closed her legs, shifted so her knees were bent in a comfortable position.

They watched the rest of the movie with her head still on a pillow in his lap. When it was over, he lifted her up, kissed her cheek, and said he'd pick her up at two on Saturday.

She hugged the front door as she watched him walk to his car. Because if she let go, she'd race after him and tell him to stay.

• • •

Bryce got home to his and Danny's place and immediately hit the shower. He'd never been more turned on in his life than he was sitting with Honor on the couch and making her feel good. Hearing the breathless sounds she made when she came had made him harder than a steel drum. If there hadn't been a pillow in his lap offering some barrier, he doubted he would've been able to reign himself in.

He knew he'd crossed a line and was treading on dangerous ground. Cooper had made it clear he didn't want Bryce near his sister, but with her blond hair, blue-gray eyes, killer bod, and naughty smile, no guy in his right mind could look away. Look closer—something Bryce couldn't stop doing—and there was a woman with much more to offer than a beautiful view. She had substance and sincerity and hated anyone studying her too hard. Which stupidly only made him want to know more.

What started nine months ago wasn't over despite his mind's protests.

He toweled off, pulled a pair of sweats on, and headed to the kitchen for a cold drink. He'd keep this unwanted connection with Honor casual because stopping didn't appeal to him. It felt good being around her and he hadn't felt good in a long time.

"Feel better?" Danny asked from the living room. His laptop sat open beside him on the couch and one of those home improvement shows played on their flat screen.

"Much." Bryce guzzled down some milk, wiped his mouth.

"Quit drinking from the carton you douche."

Bryce ambled to the oversized chair beside the couch and sat, his douche smile firmly in place.

Danny rolled his eyes. After almost three years of living together the guy should get over it already. "If you say the word 'cooties' I'm going to punch you."

"What's up your ass tonight?"

"Nothing."

"Maybe *you* should jack-off in the shower." Bryce leaned back, put his feet up on the coffee table. "Really takes the edge off."

"Do I want to know?"

"No." Bryce didn't want to lie to his best friend. Danny had more restraint than anyone he knew and taking things as far as he had with Honor tonight showed zero restraint. His actions also effed up his relationship with Cooper.

Danny's phone vibrated with a text. He picked it up and read the message. A heavy-duty frown took over his expression.

"Something wrong?" Bryce asked.

"It's Olivia. She's upset about some stuff with work." He double-thumbed a message back. "I think I'm going to head home this weekend to see her."

Olivia was the unofficial fourth Musketeer. Home was the small beach town a couple hours north where he, Danny, Zane, and Olivia had grown up. Liv lived next door to Danny, but it wasn't until sixth grade when a girl called her Chubby Livvy and Danny defended her that they all became friends.

More tomboy than girlie, she'd liked to be outdoors as much as they had.

"She didn't say anything at the wedding."

Danny kept his phone in his hand and looked up. He'd been closest to Olivia, and felt responsible for her even when he wasn't close by. "She hadn't realized how bad it would get. And she didn't want to be a downer on Zane's big day. I'll probably head out tomorrow. Be back Sunday night."

A picture of Honor immediately flashed through Bryce's mind. Naked and in his bed. Naked and in his shower. Naked and standing with her palms on the floor to ceiling window right over there. She'd love the view of the ocean and the Santa Monica pier from their high-rise condo. He'd love staring at her.

"Dammit, Bishop," Danny said.

Bryce blinked away his impure thoughts. "What?"

"Do not screw things up with Cooper."

It sucked having a friend who could read your mind, but the reprimand cleared his head. He couldn't get physical with Honor again. Coop meant too much to their agency. His inconvenient attraction aside, Bryce felt a true kinship with the skateboarder. At sixteen, a car had hit Bryce while riding his bike. With traumatic breaks in both legs, doctors doubted he'd walk again without a limp. That prognosis only made him want to prove them wrong. So he had.

"I've got this," Bryce said.

Danny scraped a hand over his jaw. "I'm not so sure."

"Win or go home, right? I haven't put everything I've got into this agency to blow a deal over a girl."

"There's the guy who swore off women."

"He's still here." He'd triumphed over every setback that fate sent his way and this time would be no different.

· · ·

Two days later, Bryce parked his car at the Los Angeles Pottery Show and hurried around to open Honor's door. He'd almost canceled their Saturday plans, but as she continued to talk about pottery and other antiques without taking a breath he was glad he hadn't. Her extensive knowledge of design and workmanship kept him fascinated, but listening to her uninhibited enthusiasm, he realized he'd hit on her main passion and she glowed with happiness. "You really know your stuff," he said.

"It's kind of my thing." She pursed her lips and her gaze took a faraway turn, as if she'd caught herself off guard with the remark.

"We never talked price. What does someone with your vast knowledge and exceptional charisma charge?"

"Hmm…" She tapped her fingers to her mouth. A mouth he could tell she tried to keep from being affected by his compliment. "Let's see how our luck goes and then I'll let you know."

"I'm already the luckiest guy here."

"Bryce."

He really got off on the sexy-sweet way she said his name, a touch of annoyance layered at the tail end, like a little emphasis on the "ssss" would scare him off. It should. But somehow he found himself walking a tightrope without a net and rather than worry about falling, a buzz ran through his veins. "Yeah?"

"You need to stop. This is work. I have to stay focused and I can't do that when you say nice things to me."

"Got it. I'll stay quiet, rely on head nods, the occasional hand gesture, and let you do your thing."

"Thank you."

Every person they met on the conference room floor of the convention center fell in instant like with Honor, making it easy for Bryce to stand back and watch. Her warmth and positive energy charmed men and women alike. She treated everyone like an old friend whether they had something of interest or not. A couple of the dealers had sold to her before and one of them had a piece of Roseville Bryce wanted.

He made eye contact with Honor and nodded to let her know his interest. His mom had over two dozen pieces, but he didn't recognize the design on this particular pot.

She picked up the Roseville. "This pattern is called Normandy. It was introduced in 1928 and its Italianate design features knots of vines, berries, and leaves on a textured background." She ran her hands over the pot, and her teacher voice had him in need of *a lot* of lessons that had nothing to do with antiques. "This was a short lived line so there aren't a lot of pieces. It's in excellent condition with only minor discoloration to the inside." She handed it to Bryce. "How much?" she asked the dealer.

"For you? Two hundred sixty-five," the older man answered.

"Do you mind if I talk to my client in private for a moment?" The man gave a nod and stepped away. "What do you think?" She smoothed her fingers over a vine on the piece. Their hands brushed and their eyes immediately met.

"I like it, but you're the expert."

Her face lit up. "It's a fair price and from what you told me of your mom's collection, I think this will be a great addition."

"Sold."

She clapped her hands together before carefully taking the pot from him and giving it to the dealer to wrap up. "That was fun," she whispered.

Bryce wrapped his arm around her waist and brought her to his side. "It was."

Her body relaxed under his hold. She laid her head on his shoulder. "Mind if we look around a little longer? I'd like to buy one or two things for the store while we're here."

"Sure." He didn't want the comfortable vibe they'd struck to end just yet.

She pulled back and like so many times before, her smiling eyes met his and he couldn't look away. She slayed him with the undisguised emotion he'd learned she didn't give away easily. Some people wore their hearts on their sleeves, but not Honor. She wore hers in the silver blue depths staring back at him.

Sometime later while driving away from the show, he slowed when he caught sight of a tattoo parlor. Without thought, he pulled over and parked in front of the shop.

"What are you doing?" she asked, her attention out the windshield.

"Getting a tattoo."

Her eyebrows shot up. "Really?"

"Yeah. You're welcome to get one, too, if you want. No pressure, though."

She gave a tiny, dubious shake of her head. She wasn't fooled. "How long have you wanted a tattoo?"

"What makes you think I don't already have one?"

"You're about as clean cut as they come, Bryce Bishop. And I've seen you…" She clamped her mouth shut.

He turned to face her more fully. "Almost naked?"

"Yes. So unless you've got your mama's face stamped to your butt cheek, I'm betting there's no ink to be found."

He grinned and leaned over the center console. "I may be clean cut on the outside, but make no mistake." He moved even closer, close enough to see her pulse jump at the base of her neck. "I like to get very, very dirty when nobody's looking."

"That's unfortunate," she whispered, angling her head so her lips were at his ear. "I bet you're fun to watch."

He threw his head back and laughed. "I'll prove it to you later."

"You think so?" She undid her seatbelt and reached for the door handle.

Bryce caught her arm. ""I'm not thinking at all."

Her lashes swept down and lifted only halfway, her focus somewhere on the dashboard. "Noted." She climbed out of the car. He came around the hood and picked up her hand. Her clammy palm almost slipped right through his. "You can do this," he said.

"As much as I want to believe I'd do it on my own, I'm not sure I would. I'm kind of mad at Payton right now."

"Ever think…" He cut himself off. He may be trying to rationalize the list to himself, but Honor didn't need to be dragged into the hit his ego had taken. He was already laying himself a little too bare, trusting Honor when his track record with women said that was a stupid move.

"Think?"

*Payton wanted to push* you *out of your comfort zone?* That maybe the list was as much about Honor as it was about her friend. "Nothing. Let's do this. How about you go first? That way you don't have to worry about it for too long."

"Can you just strap me to the chair and do it?"

"*I* can definitely do that, but not anyone else." He nudged her earlobe with his nose and breathed her in. She smelled all sorts of good.

The corner of her mouth lifted. "Maybe if you talk dirty to me, I won't think about the needle digging into my skin."

"Sweetheart, I'll do whatever you need."

"You would, wouldn't you?" She squeezed his hand a little tighter. The tiny gesture of thanks was one more reason he couldn't stay away from her.

"Every time." He'd stepped this deep into the waters and apparently he didn't know when to stop. Or if he could. He hated the thought of any other man taking care of her needs. Stupid, since the main purpose here was to help her follow through with her promise to Payton, not bond over getting inked. If anything, she seemed determined to keep an emotional distance from him, too. Just as Payton had done when she dumped him without a word.

Honor let go of his hand and pushed open the door to the tattoo parlor. "This time works."

"This time?"

"I helped you get a gift for your mom. You're helping me cross something off Payton's list. After this I say we're even and there's no reason to keep seeing each other."

Bryce flinched. At least Honor gave him some warning.

# Chapter Seven

Honor's entire body trembled. And it had almost nothing to do with the needle about to puncture her skin.

"The inside of your wrist is a great place to do this," Ryder, the tattoo artist said, holding her hand, palm up. "I don't go very deep into the skin—about 1/16 of an inch—so you'll hardly know you're being touched. The process is more irritating than anything else, like a hot vibrating sensation."

She squeezed her lips together to keep from giggling like a nervous teenager. Ryder could no doubt feel her shaking, but it was the hot vibrating sensation in her other hand giving her the most trouble. Bryce's fingers were laced with hers and his thumb kept rubbing across her other wrist.

"Remember it's all in the mind," Bryce said. "Think about how bad you want this."

Sitting in a black leather chair that unfortunately did not include any restraining devices, she held her head to the side, her cheek pressed into the chair back, chin tucked close to her shoulder, eyes on Bryce, and did just that.

She also tried not to think about how bad she wanted *him*.

"Everyone has a different threshold for pain," Ryder continued, his throaty voice a perfect match to his muscled, tattooed body. "Feeling apprehensive is normal. Even guys my size with multiple tats get nervous. It's the body's natural defense and endorphins kick in. The first minute is usually the worst and then you'll realize it's not that bad and relax."

Honor nodded. "Let's do it."

"Here goes," Ryder said.

Bryce didn't flinch when she squeezed his hand tighter than she'd ever squeezed anything before in her life. Since the moment she'd sat in the chair, his eyes had been on hers. He'd kept her with him, kept her *right there* like it was just the two of them. His eyes said even more than his words. They said *you've got this*. They said *you've got me*.

She couldn't compare his attention to any relationship she'd had before. Guys didn't stay. They played and left. That's how she worked it, wanted it. If she never committed, she'd never let anyone down. No one would get hurt. Living up to the kind of love her parents had was something she'd never accomplish.

But Bryce seemed intent on getting to know her, not forgetting her.

It scared her to think about letting his friendship go. If he weren't holding her hand and staring into her eyes with care and warmth, she would not be sitting in a tattoo parlor right now following through on one of Payton's wishes.

It freaked her out more to think about keeping him around. Despite her best efforts, her heart had gone and gotten involved. Would Payton approve? Did Honor deserve to feel something good for a little while?

Tiny beads of sweat rolled down her sides. The tattoo gun made a high-pitched buzzing sound, like an electric razor, and she tried to tune it out. She pressed her feet into the footrest on the chair. Instead of thinking a needle punctured her skin, she pictured a tiny pin pushing down and dragging across her skin.

"You're doing great," Bryce said. "Tell me why Faith?"

Since reading Pay's list, she'd given a lot of thought to the kind of tattoo she wanted and it always came back to *Faith*—the simple, yet meaningful word tattooed in a thin, handwriting font.

"It's Payton's middle name." And maybe, just maybe, having the word inked on her skin would renew her trust and confidence in herself. "It's not a bad word to live by either."

"No, it's not. I'm a pretty badass wordsmith, and I like it."

Honor squinted. "You're telling me you have a way with words?" He did. He so did. But she'd get a second tattoo before she confessed that.

His lips curled into an irresistible challenge. "Let's play a game. I'll give you a word and you tell me the definition. We'll take turns until one of us doesn't know the meaning."

"Okay." Her dad had drilled new words into her every night for months before the SAT. Not to mention she'd won the poetry slam in college.

"Ladies first."

"Collywobbles." She relaxed her hold on his hand, Ryder's pinpricks not so bad anymore.

"Stomach pain or queasiness." He scooted back into his director's chair in an obvious attempt to show her he could do this all night. "Bumbershoot."

She lifted her cheek from the chair and angled her head sideways. "An umbrella. Wabbit."

"That's not your Elmer Fudd impression is it?"

"No smartass, it isn't." The muscles in her legs loosened as her feet eased up on the footrest.

Ryder cleared his throat. "That's good. You need to take this guy down, Honor."

Bryce let out a fat-chance huff. "Wabbit means exhausted

or worn out. Unless you're in a Bugs Bunny cartoon. Then it means rabbit." He smirked. "Hootenanny."

"A country or folk music get together." Honor let out an untroubled breath. "Bishop, you're making this too easy." She ran her thumb back and forth over his, their fingers still entwined. "Fard."

"Repeat the word please."

Honor chuckled. "This isn't a spelling bee, but you look really cute all serious, so I'll give this to you as your one free pass. Fard." She pictured Bryce as a young boy dressed in a collared shirt and vest, listening to his English lessons in earnest.

"I won the spelling bee."

She laughed harder. "Of course you did."

He glared, but she felt it like the sun peeking between clouds. If he only knew how much his brains turned her on. "Face paint." She opened her mouth to protest, but he rushed to add, "Or make-up."

"Right," she said.

"Ecdysiast," he tossed out.

Crap. Was that even a real word? How was it spelled? She wouldn't put it past him to mess with her. He didn't like losing. But she didn't want to ask for clarification and see a smug look cross his gorgeous face. She closed her eyes, breaking eye contact for the first time since she'd sat down and racked her brain for an answer.

"Need a hint?" he goaded.

When pigs flew. She repeated the word to herself. Think, Honor. Given the suffix, the word referred to some kind of person. That left only a few *hundred* choices. Maybe thousands.

He brought her hand to his mouth and kissed her knuckles. She opened her eyes to find him waggling his eyebrows. *Well?* his expression said.

"Snollygoster," she mumbled.

Bryce laughed. "Oh, I can be trusted on this. You think I'd try and cheat my way to winning? No way. Give up?"

"I actually know this one," Ryder said.

Honor swung her head to look at him. She'd been staring at Bryce and paying zero attention to her tattoo artist for so long her neck kinked. "Ow." She rubbed her nape. Her gaze dropped from Ryder's face to her wrist. He'd just finished the tattoo.

*Faith*

"All done," Ryder said. He wiped the tattoo with some kind of soap, and then applied a thin coat of anti-bacterial ointment.

"I'm done," she quietly gushed.

Bryce stood and cupped the back of her neck, pushing her fingers aside to massage the painful spot. "Congratulations. You did it."

She stared up at him and emotion clogged the back of her throat. "Thank you," she whispered.

"The only thing I did was take your mind off it."

She reached up and took his hand, pressed her lips to his warm skin. "You win."

"I think we'll call this one a draw," he said, nodding toward her new tattoo.

Ryder wrapped her wrist in a plastic wrap bandage and fixed it in place with medical tape. "You can remove this in four to six hours," he said. "Now to ecdysiast."

"Okay, lay it on me," Honor said.

The two men exchanged a quick glance. "Stripper," they said in unison. Ryder put up his fist for a tap before wheeling his stool away.

She'd never heard a more enthusiastic declaration. Bryce bent his head down until his mouth brushed her ear. "How about you be my ecdysiast later tonight?"

Her pulse went into overdrive. "You have a pole?" she

whispered back, making sure to skim her lips along the smooth skin of his jaw.

"You know how to use one?" He bit her ear lobe. The sting vibrated through her, settling at the tips of her breasts.

"I'm very good at putting a rod between my legs."

He groaned and pulled back just enough for her to see an intense flare of heat in his eyes. "Think I'll skip my tattoo and take you home with me right now." He stepped away from her chair to talk to Ryder.

"There's no rush," she called once his announcement sank in. The flirting she could handle. Being alone with him at his place after the orgasm he'd given her the other night was a whole other story.

She couldn't make up her mind what do with him.

That wasn't exactly true. It terrified her what she wanted to do—to be—with him. But he deserved better than a girl who had no implicit trust in relationships. Bryce was an all or nothing guy, and she only gave pieces of herself.

"Speak for yourself," he called back.

"We're already here. You should get inked while we're here." Brilliant response, Honor. Like he was clueless about his whereabouts.

He ignored her, spoke with and paid Ryder, and had a hand on her lower back to escort her out of the shop thirty seconds later. His hands were weapons. Weapons of mass persuasion. With every touch her body craved to comply with anything and everything he suggested.

The sun had long ago set and a sliver of moon hung in the dark sky. Bryce opened the car door for her before getting into his own seat.

"I'm really proud of you," he said.

"I owe you money," she answered because his praise did funny things to her stomach and... "Thank you," she amended because she didn't like that she'd sounded rude and ungrateful. "I am feeling pretty pleased with myself at the moment. I can't believe I was so worried about this. It hurt, but not that much." She twisted to face him. "Payton's forever in my heart, and now she's forever part of my outward expression too. I'm really happy you dragged me here."

"Dragged?"

"Okay, brought. And bought. I do want to pay you back."

He put the key in the ignition. "I'll send you my bill and acceptable payment methods."

A nervous laugh bubbled up inside her as she pictured some methods she'd like to offer. *Get your mind out of the gutter.*

Reaching for her seatbelt, she focused on the happiness inside her. "I want to bask in this feeling for a while. If Payton were here, she'd be really happy. We had this ritual when one of us did something memorable. Good, bad, somewhere in the middle, it didn't matter. If it made us stop and think we celebrated it."

Bryce pulled away from the curb. "She often wrote down inspirational or funny quotes and folded them up into small slips of paper I'd find in my pants pockets."

"Really?" Honor said with a smile.

His gaze remained out the windshield. "Yeah. She also liked to read Los Angeles magazine, but only on Sunday mornings, and pick somewhere new for us to grab breakfast."

"She hated to cook."

He nodded. "Tell me about your ritual."

Honor brought a knee up and hugged her shin. "We'd make a blanket fort in front of the TV, eat graham crackers with peanut butter, drink sparkling apple cider out of champagne glasses, and find the cheesiest movies to watch until we fell asleep." She let out a breath. "It was the best."

She laid her chin atop her knee and ran a finger over her bandaged wrist. "Now as my memories fade, I'll always have this." Thanks in no small part to him. "I know you had other ideas, but do you think you could take me home? I'd like to honor our tradition tonight."

"Sure," he said, disappointment, but mostly relief in his tone. She took in his profile, his firm grip on the steering wheel. They'd both just dodged a bullet.

• • •

Honor put her paint roller back in the white plastic pan and studied the wall in her antique shop. She could scratch Painter off her list of skills and may actually need to *hire* someone to paint since her brother had bailed on her for a skateboarding tournament. A tournament he stood poised to win by the number of exclamation points in his text earlier. She hated herself for wishing he'd lose a competition so he'd rethink the agent thing. Put off going pro for a while longer. He'd liked the agent in LA. He liked Bryce. Whenever she thought about that, she disliked them both.

She raised her hands and snapped her fingers. Nope. No magic happening with the wall. Dammit. Maybe no one would notice it once she had everything else in place.

"Knock, knock," Sophie called out.

Honor turned and almost burst out laughing as her friend walked through the door.

"What?" Sophie put a hand on her hip. "The overalls too much? You said you were painting so I thought I'd help."

"You do make one heck of a poster girl for painting." Honor crossed the room and took the bag Sophie had in her other hand. "And you're the greatest friend ever for bringing lunch. Thank you."

Honor waved for Sophie to follow and strode over to her desk. She moved aside some stuff and put the bag from the Beach Café down.

Sophie practically skipped behind her. She'd been walking on Cloud Nine since returning from her honeymoon. "What color is that?"

"Eggplant." Honor pulled out a napkin and laid it on the desk before taking out the burgers and fries. Sophie grabbed her food and they found a relatively clean spot on the floor to sit down and eat.

"I like it. Are you painting the other walls the same?"

"No. Just that one." She liked things slapdash. Made her feel at home. "How's the new piano?" The surprise from Zane had floored Sophie.

"Amazing. I'm in love after only one lesson."

"Hello?" a man said from the direction of the open front door.

Honor looked up. "Danny?" He looked around like he'd heard her but couldn't see her, and she realized there were several boxes in the way. She stretched up and leaned to the side. "We're down here."

His eyes met hers. "Hey. Am I interrupting?" He stepped into the store, his attention wandering around the space.

"No. We're just eating lunch."

"Hi Danny!" Sophie said, lifting her arm higher than the box at her back and waving.

He responded in kind, then said, "Nice place you've got here. I noticed the downstairs is vacant." He stopped in the middle of the room and scuffed the floor with his work boot.

Hold on. She'd never seen Danny in anything less than slacks and dress shirts. "Mr. Case hasn't rented it yet. What are you doing here?"

Hands in the front pockets of his jeans, he studied the floor for a moment. "Bryce asked me to stop by. He told me you were fixing the place up on your own and your floors could use some sanding. I had a free couple of days, so here I am."

Sophie kept eating her burger like this was the most natural thing in the world to have Danny show up and sand floors. Honor popped to her feet. "Bryce thought you could come over here because…?"

"I'm pretty good at this sort of thing. I make a hobby of woodworking."

Honor sighed. She hadn't heard from Bryce in two weeks except via text a couple of times. He'd thanked her again for helping him with the gift for his mom and mentioned he'd had to leave town to meet with clients.

She glanced down at the floor. It did need help. But that wasn't why her heart pounded. Bryce had been thinking about her. Lord knew she hadn't stopped thinking about him. His last text, *You should let me help you take care of that one night thing*, was burned into the back of her brain. She'd yet to reply.

"So, I'll go get my stuff out of the car and be back in a few to get started. That cool?" Danny said when she'd stood there tight-lipped.

"That's fine!" Sophie responded.

Danny gave a nod and a smile and left. Honor dropped down to the floor and gave her friend the stink eye. Although, truthfully there wasn't a lot of irritation behind it.

"What do you know that I don't?" Honor asked, grabbing a few French fries.

"Nothing. But Bryce obviously wants to do something nice for you. And Danny is really good with his hands." Honor raised her eyebrows. "Stop it. I've seen some of the furniture he's made and it's beautiful." She wrapped up the remains of her burger. "According to Zane, he hasn't been himself lately, so maybe this project is something he could use, too."

Honor pressed her hands into her lap. This went beyond one-night and Payton's list territory.

"I know there's a lot going on in that head of yours." Given that Sophie used to do brain research, sometimes Honor got the feeling her friend could actually see right through her forehead and into her thoughts. "But if it's about Payton, she's gone, Honor. Feeling some guilt for being here when your friend isn't is normal, but a lot of time has passed now. I've seen you and Bryce together. There's something there. I don't think your best friend would begrudge you finding out what that is."

Gathering up their trash, Honor stood. "You're right."

Sophie got to her feet, too, and wiped her hands down the legs of her overalls. "Why do I hear a 'but' coming?"

"Buuut…" Honor smiled. "That something is very short-lived. Trust me."

Doubt clouded Sophie's eyes before she nodded. "Since we need to get out of here for Danny, want to go shopping? I could use your help with some new clothes."

"You are the only girl I know who wants to shop after scarfing down a burger and fries. I'd love to."

"Meet me at Ivy Bleu?" The small boutique had become Sophie's favorite, too.

"I'll be right behind you." Honor looked around the large room at all the boxes and small furniture pieces. Should she haul everything downstairs? Push the boxes into the corners?

Text Bryce and thank him? Tell him yes.

Danny appeared in the doorway holding a big round tool thingie. "I'm using the space below to hold some of my larger items," she said. "Should we put everything down there?"

"I got it. You take off. Just leave me the keys. If you're okay with it, I'll hang on to them and be back tomorrow. I should be done by the end of the day."

"Sounds good. Thank you." She looked around her desk for the keys and handed them to him. "A lot of the items in the boxes are fragile."

"No manhandling the boxes, got it." His eyes sparkled

and Honor got the feeling he *was* really excited about this.

"Okay, then. I'll stop by tomorrow." She stepped around him. "You like fritters?"

"Does a horse like hay?"

Honor smiled. On her walk to Ivy Bleu's she pulled her phone out of her pocket. She and Bryce were at an impasse and the ball was in her court. Sophie was right. Time marched on. People changed and made progress toward something better. Honor needed to stop standing in her own way. She'd said goodbye to eleven months since Payton's death. And the more time she spent with Bryce, the more her heart opened to him.

Both as a friend and maybe as something more, if only for one night. They both deserved to move forward and Payton would be okay with that. Her best friend had never begrudged someone else's happiness.

*Okay*, she texted.

Her phone chirped two seconds later. *Okay what? Just want to be clear since several days have passed since my offer.*

*Okay to one night. And thanks for sending me Danny.*

*Happy to help. With both. Danny's not for the taking btw.*

A flash of heat whipped through her at his possessive and flirtatious answer. She waited a beat before texting back. *That's not what he said.*

*WHAT DID HE SAY?*

She giggled at his use of all caps. *Something about keeping my keys and—*

*I'm going to kill him.*

*Now? I'd like to make good use of those hands of his first.*

*The only hands allowed to touch you are mine.*

A shot of pleasure hit between her thighs as she remembered his hands and where they'd been. Good grief. He was turning her on as she walked down Main Street.

"Honor, dear, are you all right?" cute little dyed-blond Mrs. Landry asked, bringing Honor to a stop on the sidewalk. "You look a little flush."

Of course someone would choose this moment to pass by. "I'm fine. Just worked up a little sweat painting. Thank you, though."

"You should drink more water. Doctor Flynn says it's the best thing for you. He also told me that being well hydrated helps keep the libido in good working order." She double-winked, and Honor tried to keep a straight face.

"I'll be sure to remember that." And try to forget where she heard it. The last thing she wanted to hear about was Mrs. L.'s libido when the woman liked to sneak around with Uncle Tuck.

"When is your new store opening?"

"Soon."

Mrs. L. patted her arm. "I hope so."

Honor's phone chirped. "Gotta go, Mrs. L." She hurried around the spry senior and focused back on her phone.

*Did I scare you away?*

*No. Sorry. Ran into Mrs. Landry and got schooled on the importance of drinking water.*

*So back to my hands on you, then.*

*I'm not sure your hands need to be involved.*

*Too late, sweetheart.*

*What makes you think I want a repeat performance?* She did. She wanted his hands on her again and again and again.

*The sexy sounds you made when you came.*

Her pulse sped up.

*This time I'm going to make you come with my hand, my mouth, and while buried deep inside you.*

She darted down a small alleyway and leaned against the building, pressed her legs together. *In that order?*

*Now what fun would it be to give that away?*

*How do you know I like surprises?*

*Let me surprise you tomorrow night.*

*Coop is out of town.*

*I'll be over at 8.*

Her stomach fluttered and her head got a little light. She'd led him to her front door, she couldn't back out now. *Okay.*

*I can't wait.*

The flutters moved upward and filled her heart. She left the texting at that, so delighted by his admission that her hands shook. She couldn't wait either.

• • •

Bryce dropped his phone next to him on the couch and stared at the email on his laptop. Cooper Mitchell needed more time to make a decision and would be in touch soon. Honor Mitchell had made her decision and tomorrow night they'd be doing a lot more than touching.

Whether or not it was the right thing to do, he'd find out later. The fact that she trusted him made him forget about his own trust issues. She couldn't hurt him if he kept this about the list.

And until he signed Cooper, he saw no reason not to be with her. She didn't want a relationship, but she wanted a one night stand. No strings attached sex meant no emotional entanglement.

Really Cooper should be thanking him. Bryce guaranteed Honor got exactly what she wanted and deserved. A good guy who respected her body and wishes. A guy who would worship her and make her feel safe while he rocked her world.

*You're an idiot if you think your emotions aren't involved.*

His mind wandered to Payton. He'd cared deeply for her, but over the past several weeks he'd come to realize he hadn't truly loved her. Not the way he'd wanted to love someone. She'd never sparked the kind of intensity needed for forever. Coming to that understanding, he'd made his offer to Honor.

He couldn't stop thinking about her. She tied him in knots of lust and affection and he wanted to make tomorrow night good for her. A part of him planned to love her with slow, smooth strokes like he'd done on her couch a couple of weeks ago. But another part of him wanted to spread her legs wide and pound into her with unrestrained urgency so she'd know exactly how crazy she made him.

So he'd do both.

And give her a night she'd always remember before he walked away

# Chapter Eight

"I don't think you should drive in this weather," Honor said into her cell. She did not have cold feet. She just didn't think it nice of Mother Nature to drop the rainstorm to end all rainstorms on her Friday night plans.

"You think a little rain is going to keep me away from you?" Bryce said, his voice warmer and more delicious than her favorite hot chocolate.

Damn him.

She drew her legs up onto the couch and tucked the blanket around her. "I'm sure the roads are a mess and it's only supposed to rain harder."

Okay, so she had lukewarm feet. She'd reminded herself all day this was just sex, yet she knew that was a lie. She'd agreed to sleep with Bryce because she cared about him.

Not part of the ONS rules, Ms. Mitchell.

"You worried about me?"

"Maybe," she half whispered. Her stomach had been twisted in a troublesome knot since the downpour hit at five o'clock. Her father had been in a terrible accident on a rainy night when she was little and she'd never forgotten the trip to the hospital, her mom's hand tight around hers, her eyes red from tears she wouldn't let fall in front of Honor.

"Thanks," he said, like no one had worried about him in a while. "But nothing is going to keep me from you."

She liked that. She liked it a lot. But… "I'm not going anywhere," she said. "You should stay put and we'll do this when the weather is better." It wasn't like she had any other one night stands lined up.

The doorbell sounded. Oh no. She hoped her neighbor's yard wasn't flooding like the last time it had rained this hard.

"You want me to stay put?" Bryce asked.

"Yes." Honor jumped to her feet. "It's really storming here." Rain hit the windows in a loud, steady beat. "Hang on a sec, there's someone at my door."

Someone tall, dark and drop-dead handsome. Her legs shook at the sight of him. "You're here," she breathed into the phone before dropping her arm and taking him in. He was over an hour early, but he'd made it, safe and sound. She flung herself at him.

He wrapped her in his arms, his big, strong body curling around hers, and in that moment she knew. Knew she was in way over her head, but she couldn't stop it.

"Hi." His mouth brushed her temple and he inhaled, breathing her in.

She hung on to him until a sharp whistle of wind sent a chill down her body and she pulled back. "Come inside."

"Someone told me I had to—"

She cut him off with a quick kiss, sexy stubble tickling her lips. "Hurry."

The naughty play on his lips made it impossible not to smile in return. He moved around her. "Yes, ma'am."

"How long have you been standing outside my door?" She took his jacket and hung it on the antique coat rack she'd bought last year.

"I didn't think it possible," he said, ignoring her question and taking a strand of hair at her shoulder between his fingers, "but you've gotten prettier since the last time I saw you."

Definitely over her head. Especially when she stared up at him and saw the most incredible face she'd ever laid eyes on. That dimple in his chin alone made it hard to breathe, made it hard to talk.

She brushed by him to give herself a few seconds to regroup without his seductive eyes on her. Didn't entirely work because she felt him watching her backside. And crap. She glanced down at her yoga pants and sweatshirt. Since he'd arrived early she hadn't changed yet. Not that she had her entire closet of clothes piled on her bed because she didn't know what to wear for him or anything.

The evidence of her indecision layered around her room embarrassed her just thinking about it. She spun around. "Can you give me a minute to, uh, change?"

He took her hand, turned it over, and rubbed his thumb over her pulse. Over *Faith*. "There's no reason to be nervous around me, Honor. I got here early because I couldn't wait to see you, but if you're having second thoughts I can go."

All this nervous tension wasn't something she was used to. And now with his considerate words and insanely arousing touch, he zapped her of any semblance of control. He made her both unsure and certain at the same time.

"I don't want you to go."

"How about we eat something and talk first, then?"

"That sounds good." She took a step back and turned toward the kitchen. "I'll make us my special grilled cheese sandwiches."

"I happen to love grilled cheese sandwiches. Want some help?"

"That's okay. I've got it." She grabbed the frying pan

and needed ingredients. "Did you, uh, have a good day?" she asked. And instantly regretted the inquiry. It made her sound like his girlfriend, not his one night stand. But he had brought up talking and that was the first thing to pop into her head.

He leaned against the counter and watched her. "I did. Spent the morning on the phone finalizing a couple of client appearances, then had a lunch date. Mind if I grab a drink?"

"Date, huh? Was she pretty?" she tossed the question out like it wasn't a big deal. In reality, her heart caved at the thought he might be on the brink of seeing someone.

"What? No." He stepped away from her fridge. "You don't honestly think I'd be here if it was that kind of lunch, do you?"

Honor shrugged.

His warm hands squeezed her upper arms, his chest pressed against her back, and his mouth hovered below her earlobe. "You're the only woman I'm seeing, Honor. The only one I can't stop thinking about."

There he went with those words again. She had zero defenses against them. Red-hot prickles danced over her skin as her sweatshirt slid off one shoulder.

"If you knew the dirty dreams I've been having about you…" His lips feathered over the curve of her neck down to her bared shoulder.

She closed her eyes and practically melted into him. Her nipples pebbled into tight, achy points, a rush of heat filled her tummy and spread lower. Even though one night didn't constitute any kind of obligation, Bryce gave it to her. At least for right now.

"Ow! Frick." Her eyes flew open as she whipped her arm back from the stovetop and shook her hand furiously back and forth.

Bryce stumbled back. "You burned yourself?" She nodded. "Let's get it under cold water." He turned on the faucet and pushed up her sleeve just before she thrust her hand under the spray. "Sorry," he mumbled, like a little boy who'd been caught with his hand in the cookie jar.

"You should be," she teased. "You distracted me from what I was doing."

He reached around her back and turned off the knob for the burner. That would teach her to let the pan warm up before she was really ready.

"You've been distracting me since the moment our eyes met."

She purposely focused her gaze on her burned fingers, afraid he'd see how much he affected her, too.

"Hey." He tucked his finger under her chin and guided her face toward his. "Did I say something wrong?"

"No." She turned off the faucet and dried her hand with a paper towel. "I really do want to cook for you, though, so sit at the table and let me do my thing."

"You all right?" he asked, nodding at her hand.

"Fine." She waved him off and cooked her special grilled cheese sandwiches—cheddar cheese, bacon, alfalfa sprouts, and ranch dressing on sourdough.

While they ate, they talked about everything and nothing and she relaxed. He'd mentioned he liked hearing her voice, but she could listen to him talk all day. His smooth, deep sound, full of confidence and sincerity touched down to places inside her no one else had reached.

"Middle name?" Bryce asked.

Being with Bryce was so easy she didn't mind his onslaught of questions. "Rosalie. Yours?"

"Honor Rosalie Mitchell," rolled off his tongue with such reverence that he wiped out the negative implication she always associated with hearing her mom say it.

"Okay, quit stalling and give me yours."

"Aleksius." He gave the cutest squint to go along with the

disclosure. "It's a family name."

"You don't like it?" She lifted his empty plate and put it on top of hers.

"Not even a little. Football or baseball?" The sleeves of his charcoal gray ribbed cotton shirt were pushed up to his elbows and she glanced at his strong forearms and hands, imagining them handling her for a touchdown.

"Football. Cupcake or brownie?"

"Brownies plural. But if we're going to talk dessert, I know exactly what I want right now."

Honor knew, too. Yet the tiny thread of self-preservation she'd been clinging to must have shown on her face because Bryce added, "But I can be patient. You're worth the wait."

"You don't know enough about me to say that."

"I know you." He reached across the table and took her hand. "I know you care more about others than you do yourself. I know you don't pretend to be something you're not. You love your brother and movies and antiques. When you laugh your eyes sparkle like a thousand stars tucked inside a glass jar. The rain isn't your favorite thing. And you make the best grilled cheese sandwich I've ever eaten."

Her heart stopped. With a few candid words he made her feel important. Special. Worthy of someone like him. At least for the next few hours.

For seven long years she'd carried the burden of hurting Lance. Guilt and pain still weighed heavily, breaking her faith and belief that she deserved to belong with anyone. But maybe Bryce saw something in her she'd yet to see in herself. Maybe for tonight she did deserve to be swept away.

She pulled him up by their clasped hands and walking backward, led him down the hallway toward her bedroom. His unwavering stare heated her skin, the fathomless dark pools whispering he was in this 100 percent, too.

No one had ever looked at her like that before.

They stumbled into her room. She flipped the wall switch for the vintage Victorian lamp hanging from the ceiling. Soft light spilled around them.

Crap. She'd forgotten her closet had vomited clothes onto her bed.

"Hang on." With one giant sweep of her arms, she pushed all the clothes on her bed onto the floor.

He chuckled. "You'll explain that to me later."

"Maybe." She would. He had a unique effect on her, making her a bundle of nerves but willing to share all her secrets at the same time. "Now where were we?"

Bryce cupped her face in his hands and his mouth fused with hers. The kiss started slow and sensual, like a story about to begin, and Honor almost pushed him away. There was no happily ever after for her. Nothing but tonight. But then his tongue slipped inside her mouth and all she could do was lose herself to the sensations his kiss breathed into every cell of her body.

With every exceptional sweep of his tongue, she trembled and craved more. She gave as good as she got, tasting, licking, sucking. One hand held his nape, the other the back of his head to keep him firmly in place.

He broke the kiss to pull her sweatshirt over her head. She tugged his shirt up and off. From the heated gaze he directed at her chest, the lacy pale yellow bra she'd worn in anticipation of this evening met with his approval.

"You're so beautiful, Honor. So unbelievably sexy."

She traced her fingers over his chest and down to the grooves of his sculpted abdomen. "So are you. You should go shirtless all the time."

"I will if you will." He cupped her breast and trailed the pad of his thumb over the swell. Her nipples hardened, she arched into his touch.

A split second later he dipped his head and took her

into his mouth. Lost in a wave of pleasure as he sucked her through the thin material of her bra, she gripped his shoulders to keep upright.

Openmouthed kisses with his tongue and teeth moved from one breast to the other. His hands roamed up her back and with one flick of his fingers he had her bra unclasped.

"Damn," he whispered, feasting on her without any barrier. The stubble on his face scraped her skin in the most delicious way. She wiggled out of the lingerie.

Sparks skittered over her exposed flesh as he palmed her aching breasts, kneaded her, took her nipples into his hot mouth, and lavished her with flicks of his tongue and insanely potent pressure from his lips.

"God you taste good," he murmured. "Makes me wonder how good you'll taste elsewhere."

"You'd better find out," she said, her voice strained with want. Need. Desire beyond her control.

His mouth slid south and his hands got busy pulling down her yoga pants. He eyed the panties that matched her bra. "I also know your favorite color is yellow," he said.

She swallowed the lump in the back of her throat and nodded. "What's yours?"

"Honor blue." His voice, thick and raspy, she wasn't sure she heard him right. "The color of your eyes. That incredible combination of blue and gray that renders me helpless and hopeful at the same time."

So much adoration for this man crashed over her she thought she might drown.

"Hold on to me." Without waiting for her to comply, he slid her panties off and buried his face between her legs.

The urgent need she sensed from him as his tongue swept over her made her knees buckle. She dug her nails into his shoulders.

Her ragged gasps filled the room. She clung to him like

she'd die if he stopped. His lips and tongue worked in perfect sync. Every glide and flick better than the last. He devoured her like he couldn't get enough.

Anticipation welled inside her, boiling to the point of pleasurable pain so magnificent she panted, sighed, and said, "Don't stop. Please don't stop."

His fingers found her curls and he brushed her most sensitive spot with the pad of his thumb. That in conjunction with his mouth sent her spiraling into the hottest, longest orgasm of her life. She shattered and called out his name.

He scooped her up, obviously aware that his oral skills had rendered her unable to stand on her own. She nuzzled his neck until he stopped at the foot of her bed and tossed her onto the mattress. Scrambling to her knees she reached for the button and zipper of his slacks.

"I'm going to lick and taste every inch of your naked body before the night is through," he said, helping her shuck his pants.

"Okay," she said breathless, "But first I need you inside me." She sat back and watched him take off his boxer briefs. His erection, big, thick, and glorious, made her achy and wet for him all over again. She stared, unashamed. Turned on. Hot. He rolled on a condom and trapped her between the bed and his sexy body.

He lifted her arms above her head, laced their fingers together, and kissed her. His smooth, well-defined chest rubbed hers and his knee nudged her legs wider so she felt the hot press of his length at her center. He made love to her mouth, nibbling her bottom lip, teasing her tongue with his, caressing her lips with devastating tenderness and urgency.

"Look at me," he whispered as he lifted his head.

She opened her eyes and he thrust inside her. Exquisite vibrations thrummed through her body, forcing the breath from her lungs. Bryce's groan of pleasure filled her head. They didn't take their eyes off each other as he drove into her, each robust slide of his hips claiming her. Possessing her. Rocking her world.

"God, you feel good," Bryce said.

"You do, too. Better than good."

The smile he gave changed his expression from fierce and enraptured to intense and intoxicating and all of them caused her heart major damage. Then his mouth invaded hers again and she willingly gave all of her senses and thoughts over to him.

He released his hold on her hands and cupped her cheek. She wasted no time raking her fingers around his shoulders and down his back. His warm skin felt like silk and she planned to lick and taste every inch of him, too.

His lips kissed over her jaw, down her neck. He skimmed back up to her ear lobe and whispered filthy, naughty things he planned to do to her.

She hadn't known how much dirty talk could turn her on. Combined with his sexy voice it thrilled her unbearably. Her core muscles tightened, she wound her legs around his hips meeting him thrust for thrust, and she came with his name on her lips once again.

"I'm glad you like what I have in store for you," he said against her cheek before lifting her bottom with his hand and moving deeper inside her.

Catching her breath, she moaned against his continued onslaught. He didn't let up and his measured, insistent rhythm took her right back to the edge of release. "Bryce," she moaned.

"Come for me one more time." He lifted her hips higher, hitting her sensitive core at just the right angle and…

"Oh…Oh god," she shouted, convulsing around him a second time.

He followed right behind, shuddering then stiffening with

his release before he collapsed on top of her.

She was 100 percent ruined. And happier than she'd ever admit. He rolled over and tucked her against his side. "Give me a few minutes," he said, sounding tired but happy, "before I make good on my promises."

She circled his nipple with her finger. "That's a pretty short recovery time."

"You inspire me."

"Yeah?" She loved the sound of that. What she didn't love was the sound of the doorbell.

"Is that someone at—"

She bolted up. She'd been unaware of the rain while making love with Bryce, but now the incessant thrumming of the storm on her window came through loud and clear. "Yes. I think it's probably my neighbor and she needs my help."

# Chapter Nine

Rain pelted Bryce's back as he removed the wet, muddy leaves from the drain in Mrs. Jamison's backyard. His finger stung like a mother, having sliced it open when he pried the rusted metal drain cover off, but his efforts were paying off. Water ran down the pipe now rather than pooling around the opening.

The tiny, older woman had been so frantic at Honor's front door that he'd run out without shoes and barely had his pants zipped and buttoned.

He glanced up at the sliding glass door where he'd insisted Honor wait with Mrs. Jamison. Honor had her arm around the woman's shoulders and her lips moved. No doubt she spoke reassuring and caring words to her neighbor. His heart swelled with affection. Honor's regard for others was insanely attractive.

Reaching as far down as his arm could go, he scooped out the last of the caked-together leaves. Tomorrow he'd call someone to run a plumber's snake down the drain to rid any more clogs.

He stood and gave a thumbs-up, glad the water level around the small yard had dropped considerably. Mrs. Jamison put a hand to her chest in a gesture of gratitude and relief. Honor motioned with a thumb over her shoulder to meet him around front.

The warped wood side gate took some heaving to close properly and he made a mental note to mention it to Danny. His friend could have it fixed in no time.

Honor met him under the awning at the garage. Her dazzling smile made him eager to get back to her bedroom. "Mrs. Jamison says you're her hero."

He shrugged off the description before a full body shiver swept over him. "I was happy to help."

"You're freezing. Come on." She ran ahead of him to her front door. Once there she pushed him inside and straight into the bathroom where she turned on the shower.

Curious as to what exactly she had in store for him, he kept still, arms at his sides. He'd taken charge in the bedroom. Maybe she'd like to run the show here as steam filled the room. Just until he put into play the next blitz on her smoking hot body.

Her regard connected with his and the chill that had seeped under his skin disappeared. With one look she set his blood on fire. With one look he knew there was nothing casual about what they were doing. He should hightail it out of here right now, but the drawing power swirling between them had roots that defied his good sense. He'd set his mind to pulling them up in the morning.

She pulled his dripping wet shirt over his head then bent down to remove his drenched pants. She'd unbuttoned and unzipped him when her head jerked back and she started inspecting his torso. "You're bleeding somewhere." Her voice, full of concern, hit him square in the gut. "There's blood on the floor."

He lifted his arm and sure enough blood dripped down his index finger. "It's nothing."

"It's not nothing." She popped to her feet and took his wrist to tug him to the sink. With his hand over the porcelain bowl she studied the wound. "You cut it on the drain?"

"Yes."

"When was your last tetanus shot?"

The corners of his mouth lifted. Nurse Honor was damn adorable. "Hell if I know." He flinched when her fingers got a little too close to the action.

"You need stitches."

"No way."

"Way." She put his finger under the faucet and washed it with soap and warm water.

He clenched his jaw. Jesus Christ, that hurt.

"Here's what you're going to do. Jump in the shower really quick to get warm, I'll find some sweats of Cooper's for you to put on, and then I'm taking you to the ER." She turned off the water and dropped back to the floor to wrangle his pants and underwear off him.

With only one night to do all the things he planned to do to her, the last thing he wanted was to waste time with a trip to the hospital.

Her warm breath fanned over his cock and it sprang to life.

"Bryce! This is serious."

"As a hard on."

She stood, put her palm over his heart. The skin there heated. "Do what I asked and I'll take very good of that later."

Hard—no pun intended—to argue with that, especially when her sexy voice carried soft-heartedness that he felt deep in his chest. He got in and out of the shower, put on the clothes she gave him and pressed some gauze to his finger to try and stop the bleeding that refused to let up.

"Okay, let's go," she said from the bathroom doorway. She'd slipped on knee-high black rain boots with white polka dots on them and a black trench coat with a belt cinched around her waist.

"Looking at you, I want it to rain every day." He didn't hide his top to bottom perusal. Covered from head to toe she still stole his breath.

A blush fanned across her cheeks. "Quit stalling and come on." When he didn't budge, she titled her head to the side and studied him.

"I really think a Band Aid will do," he asserted.

"Trust me. It won't." She stepped closer like maybe she understood what he was really trying to say. The idea that she recognized his unspoken thoughts on the situation threw the night completely off balance. He was here for one night of sex. The last thing he wanted was her inside his head.

"How do you know?" he ventured anyway.

She gulped. "Coop's had more stitches than I've had sneezes." She ran her fingers through his damp hair. "You don't like hospitals, do you?"

"Not really." His heart hurdled to the back of his throat. She got him.

"What happened?"

"Bike accident when I was sixteen. Broke both my legs." Her eyes widened, not with sympathy, but awe. No one had any idea unless he shared it. "I don't talk about it, but if I can avoid hospitals, I do. They remind me of a rough time."

She took a deep breath and his injured hand in hers. Her gentle touch sent tingles racing down his spine. "Okay. We'll do it here."

"Do what here?"

"Stitch you up." She guided him down to sit on the closed toilet seat.

"You know how to do that?" he asked surprised.

"Yes." She took off her coat and flung it out the bathroom door. The boots followed, leaving her in yoga pants and a pale pink sweatshirt that slid off her shoulder and drove him crazy with lust.

"But you're afraid of needles."

She knelt in front of him and turned to pull a handled tray of medical supplies out of the sink cabinet. Holy shit. She was serious.

"I know. And to be honest, I've only done this on a banana."

He didn't know whether to be worried or intrigued by that. The fact that she'd even held a needle deserved some kudos. "Elaborate?"

"Coop's got this whole suture kit here because he's constantly banging himself up and rather than go to the doctor every time he needs a stitch or two, our aunt, who's a plastic surgeon, taught him how to stitch up a wound. It's crazy that he can fix himself up and be so in control of the needle. I think that's the only reason I could handle watching him do it." She tore open several sterilized pouches and lined them up on a clean towel. "One day he insisted on teaching me in case he hurt himself somewhere where he needed assistance. We used a banana to practice on."

"How'd that go?"

"I was freaked out at first, but then it went okay." Her hands shook, ever so slightly, telling him she was not okay right now.

With his good hand, he tucked a knuckle under her chin and lifted her face. Eyes glassy with emotion met his. She was scared, but determined. "I'll be fine with just a bandage, Honor."

He needed to get out of that bathroom and back into bed with her so the only thing he felt was her warm, soft skin. One night of mindless pleasure. One night to help her keep her promise and they could both move on.

"What if you're not? What if it gets infected and the infection moves into your bloodstream or something. I've seen enough of Coop's cuts to know that yours isn't superficial. I've seen…" She pressed her lips together and shut her eyes.

She'd seen her brother almost lose his life. "Sweetheart—"

"Please let me do this," she practically begged and Bryce realized this was about more than simply stitching him up or facing her fear of needles. She needed this success, this win.

"I have the utmost confidence in you." He removed the gauze and gave her his finger. The bleeding had finally stopped.

Her soft, grateful gaze collided with his and he hoped she saw he meant what he said 100 percent. He trusted her to take care of him.

"This is a topical anesthetic cream." She used a Q-tip to wipe the ointment over and around the cut. "It doesn't work quite as well as an injection so you'll definitely feel me working, but it shouldn't be too painful."

Bryce leaned back and watched Honor work. She used enough anesthetic to numb his finger for a week, but he kept quiet, knowing how worried she was about causing him any discomfort. She continued to describe her actions and he got the feeling talking helped calm her nerves.

When the time came to actually insert the needle, her chest rose and fell and even though her hand shook, he knew once she got past the first poke, her determination would carry her the rest of the way with ease.

She continued to impress him. Engage him. Everything about her made him want more. But he had to ignore it. He'd fight the feelings she stirred no matter how hard that seemed at the moment because he had no plans to risk his heart again. He might like Honor more than he should, but he had nothing to give beyond making her feel good for the next few hours.

They'd agreed to explore the attraction between them, but it ended when the sun came up.

"Bryce?" Something waved in front of his face. "Hello?" Honor said, her hand moving back and forth.

He blinked back to the present. "Sorry. Yeah?"

She pushed him in the arm. "Oh my god. Do not scare me like that! I thought you went into shock or something. You're all done." She sat back on her haunches with a big, beautiful smile on her face and just like that his pulse careened out of control.

"Thank you." He didn't look at his finger. He only looked at her. Why couldn't he look away?

"You're welcome."

"Now it's time I show you my thanks." He scooped her up into his arms, ignoring protests that she needed to clean up first, and carried her back to bed. "Congratulations, Nurse Mitchell. You've successfully passed Suturing 101 and you know that means?"

Her giggles lit a flame inside him. "I have no idea." She scooted back on the bed at the same time she pulled her sweatshirt over her head. He loved how eager she was to get naked again. "You'd better fill me in." Joy and anticipation were etched around the curve of her mouth and crinkles at the corners of her bottomless Honor blue eyes.

"I'm going to fill you all right." He stood at the edge of the bed and stripped. She pulled off the rest of her clothes. "Turn over," he instructed.

She stretched out onto her stomach, wiggled that fine ass of hers, and gazed up at him over her shoulder. Beautiful didn't begin to describe every slope and curve of her delectable body. His blood heated, every muscle tightened.

He started at her heel and worked his way up the back of her calf to her knee with openmouthed kisses. "You're so soft," he whispered. Goose bumps spread over her flesh.

"And you smell amazing." He spread her legs and licked up her inner thigh, breathing her in.

"Mmm…" she said, lifting her hips off the bed.

"Not so fast, sweetheart." His fingers splayed over her bottom and lower back, up her smooth sides. He followed the trail with his lips and tongue. She writhed and moaned, reached behind her to touch him.

When his body covered hers, his mouth at her nape, he said in a low voice, "It means you've earned the Bryce Special."

She laughed as if that were the funniest thing she'd ever heard. The bed shook with her amusement. "That's…" she let out a breath, "that's the best line of B.S. I've ever heard." She buried her face in the sheets to muffle her continued chuckles.

Yeah, he'd walked right into that one. "You think you're funny, huh?"

"I think you're funny," she sputtered.

Good thing she couldn't see the smile on his face. It would ruin his next move. He wrapped an arm around her middle and lifted her onto her knees. His erection pressed against the sweet spot between her legs. She stopped laughing.

"Remember what I whispered in your ear earlier?"

"Yes."

"It's gonna be harder now. Dirtier."

"That's good." She wiggled her behind, arched her back. "Because I want everything you've got. I want you so deep that I lose my mind."

He groaned. "Count on it."

After he'd made her lose her mind several times and the rain had stopped pounding the windows, Honor had challenged him to a game of Scrabble. One game had turned into best two out of three when she lost the first one. She kicked his ass on the next two, but he didn't care, the words they'd created and argued about had fueled another round of the hottest sex of his life.

Now, they lay nestled together atop her comforter on the floor in front of the fireplace, the game board and pieces scattered around them. The flames cast a warm glow throughout the room, but it didn't come close to capturing the radiance around her.

His sunshine on a rainy night.

He lifted up onto an elbow and gazed down at her. Her blond hair tumbled around her shoulders in a sexy mess. Scratch marks from his stubble marred her neck, collarbone, and swells of her breasts.

She cupped his cheek. "I loved your B.S." The affection in her eyes and in her tone belied her claim she had no interest in relationships.

*Fall in love.* The last item on Payton's list sprang to mind. He and Honor had talked about everything else and while he'd gotten over his initial hurt at discovering Payton might not have loved him like he'd thought she did, he wondered how the request affected Honor. She'd been mad about the tattoo. Was she angry about that, too?

He drew lazy circles on Honor's chest. "Can I ask you about the last wish on Payton's list?"

Honor's eyes widened and she quickly sat up, reaching for the blanket haphazardly lying at their feet to cover herself up. "What about it?"

He rolled onto his back and laced his hands behind his head, hoping his relaxed position would unknot the tension rolling off her in waves. "It's a big deal, and I'm assuming Payton knew how you felt about it." Had Honor ever been in love? Had someone hurt her and triggered the guard she rarely let down? Did they also have that in common?

"She did. I confided in her about everything." Honor's gaze settled on the orange-red flames in the fireplace.

"Do you want to fall in love?"

"No."

He wasn't really surprised, but he was curious. "Why not?"

She looked away. "Because I'll fail at it."

And therein lay the reason she hated to let her guard down. Bryce didn't let the risk of failure stop him from going after what he wanted. But if Honor didn't believe she deserved success, she'd never stop running from it.

• • •

Honor cracked open one eye. Sunshine seeped through the slats of the window shutters, but the last thing she wanted to do was wake up. Muscles that had never been sore before smarted in the best possible way—the multiple orgasm way. Bryce had worshipped her body from head to toe and she'd responded like never before. He'd loved her thoroughly. Completely. Naked in each other's arms, every fear, doubt, barrier between them, had ceased to exist. For a little while longer she wanted to enjoy lying on the floor wrapped up in those delicious memories.

She didn't have to roll over to know Bryce was gone. She felt his absence in the stillness, the chill at her back. They'd had their one night stand and he'd slipped away. A flutter filled her stomach and head. Best night ever, even if she'd been hoping he'd stick around for coffee.

Better he hadn't.

Her back cracked as she stretched her arms above her head. Gah. Is this what it felt like to have sex over and over again? Maybe she'd just lay here a while longer to hold on to the sensation.

Turning to her side she tucked her hands under her cheek. A tiny ember glowed in the fireplace, Scrabble pieces littered the floor, blankets, and pillows strewn about brought a small smile to her face.

A long stretch of Saturday lay before her and she had nowhere to be, but she got up and went through her morning routine. Shower. Dress. Coffee. Sitting at the kitchen table, she palmed her yellow smiley face mug and tried not to think about Bryce. She hadn't been overly talkative last night when the conversation turned to love, so afraid he would see she wasn't capable of it.

Not in the way he deserved.

The sting of rejection flared in her chest, which was stupid. She'd gotten what she wanted out of last night. No strings sex so she could cross if off Payton's list. Only the accomplishment shouldn't hurt. It shouldn't feel like she'd lost something when she never had it in the first place.

Or wanted it. She'd made sure her head knew the night meant nothing, hadn't she? Focused on Bryce's warm skin, lean muscles, perfect mouth, deft hands.

Not the man.

She finished her coffee and got to her feet. She needed to swim, needed to drift in the ocean and let the current carry away all her stupid thoughts.

Halfway down the hall to her room so she could change into her wetsuit, the doorbell rang. Her heart stopped. It wouldn't be him.

It was.

"Hey, can we come in?" Bryce said, his eyes eating her up, his smile the one she pretended he kept just for her.

"Uh, sure." She opened the door wider and let "them" in. "What are you doing here? I thought…"

He looked around her living room before walking to the kitchen to put the small aquarium in his arms down on the counter. Once his hands were also free of the white plastic bag he'd carried, he turned and almost knocked her on her butt with the pure, unfiltered joy on his face.

"First off, you were sound asleep when I woke this morning and looked so peaceful I didn't want to disturb you. That's why I left without saying anything." He took her hand in his. She had no choice but to move closer.

"And second, I did leave with every intention of driving home." His thumb stroked her knuckles. "But I can't stop thinking about you. I wish I could, but I can't. So, what I have here is a gift." He drew her to the countertop. "This is a puffer fish."

The pentagon shaped tank stood about two feet tall. Blue rocks filled the bottom. A plastic plant and treasure chest sat atop the jagged stones. The cute little fish had big eyes and a rounded body with black polka dots and fins on either side of him that fluttered like hummingbird wings.

"He's staring at me."

"He knows a beautiful thing when he sees it."

She had no answer for that. No idea what to think or feel about his admission. For the moment, she'd go with the flow.

He slid the tank closer to the wall to plug it in. The treasure chest yawned, tiny bubbles floated up. "The filter should be good for a while. Can I have a clean glass?" Honor grabbed one. He filled it with water from the tap and poured it into the tank, continuing to fill-and-pour until the water level in the tank had risen almost to the top. Next he added a couple of clear drops of liquid from a tiny plastic bottle.

"Have you ever had a fish before?"

"No. You seem pretty knowledgeable, though."

"I had my own tank for a few years when I was young." Bryce held up a small container. "This is his food. He only needs a flake or two once a day."

"Got it." She leaned closer with her elbows on the counter,

her nose almost touching the glass. "I should name him."

"You should."

"What do you think of Jaws?"

Bryce laughed. "I like it."

They watched Jaws for a couple of minutes in comfortable silence. Bryce's gesture overwhelmed her and she didn't know what to do or say next. Finally she decided on, "You bought me a pet." For some reason it seemed necessary she acknowledge that aloud.

"He's more than a pet."

She puzzled over that as she lifted up and faced him.

"He's who you can fall in love with without worry."

Her legs shook. Bryce caught her around the waist before she collapsed to the floor in a heap of love and longing and devotion.

"Whoa." He brought her flush against his hard, warm chest and abs. "You all right?"

No. She wasn't. Not by a long shot. "Bryce," she said softly.

"Honor," he answered just as quietly.

"No one…" She swallowed the emotion clogging the back of her throat. "No one has ever thought about me the way you do." He'd made her promise to Payton a real possibility. *Fall in love*, Pay had listed. Not *fall in love, get married, and have babies*. She was halfway to loving Jaws already. By tomorrow she'd be all the way there. And she'd feed him every day and talk to him every day and watch him swim every day.

If she simply took the words as Pay had written them, then she'd followed through.

"That makes us even," Bryce said, "because I've never thought about anyone the way I do you."

She lifted onto her tiptoes and kissed him. He cradled her face with his big, strong hands as hers snaked through his soft brown hair. She feasted on his lips and tongue until she had to come up for air. "Thank you," she whispered.

"My pleasure."

"Do you have plans for today?"

"That depends." He toyed with her hair and even though she knew it impossible to feel something through the fine strands, her scalp tingled.

"On?"

"What you have planned."

"I was thinking about spending the day in bed."

His eyes went all dark and seductive. The dimple in his chin deepened. "The one night stand is off the table?"

"No. But maybe we could bend the rules a little. Extend the night to include the day. Just this once." She knew it was wrong to keep him with her, to continue what they'd had into daylight hours, but she couldn't help herself. Guilt still sat in the back of her mind because she was here with Bryce and Payton wasn't, but worse was her heart and body had overruled the logic she'd come to live by since Lance. The truth she held above all else: She didn't have the capacity to truly love someone and not hurt him.

For a little while longer, though, she wanted to pretend that nothing else existed but her and Bryce.

"I'm all yours," he said with a grin, and a part of her wished that were possible.

# Chapter Ten

Early Monday morning Honor walked down Main Street toward the Beach Café to grab coffee before she hit the mayor's office. Spring Break was around the corner and she had a ton of work to do for the annual street fair.

A group of seagulls squawked overhead in the clear blue sky, drawing her attention up. It was beautiful after rainy days. The air cleaner, the sights and sounds crisper. Like living in a postcard.

She took a deep breath in through her nose and out through her mouth just before a burst of hot pink rounded the corner and she choked out a laugh. Coming at her was Midge and her "Street Team." The walking group—Midge, Mrs. Landry, Shirley, and Mrs. Jamison—all wore bright pink *Just Do It* T-shirts and the hot pink tutus they'd acquired when they power jammed through their first Color Run a few months ago. 'Power jammed' was Mrs. L.'s phrase and she made sure everyone knew it. They walked around town every morning to stay fit. Look up 'fit' in the White Strand dictionary and there was a bonus definition: keep your nose in everyone's business.

The main reason Honor giggled, though, had everything to do with the team's new leader. He'd also donned a tutu.

"Yo, Honorlicious," Dylan said, his blonde Einstein hair standing in crazier disarray than usual.

"Nice outfit." Honor came to a stop with her hands on her hips.

Dylan grinned. "Right?" He brought the group to a halt by putting his hand up, arm bent at the elbow before he leaned forward and whispered, "They're paying me so I'll wear whatever they want." Straightening he said, "I'm whipping these ladies into shape for the Cove 5K."

"That's great." Honor put up her palm to high five the team of adorable older women.

"Honor," Mrs. Jamison said, pulling her into a hug. "Please thank that boyfriend of yours again for coming to my rescue Saturday night."

"Oh, he's not —"

"And tell him he must let me repay him for sending a plumber over yesterday to put a snake in my drain."

Mrs. L. got a gleam in her eye and pressed her hands together. "Tell us again how long his snake was, Betty."

"Long. And when he bent over —"

"Whoa," Honor and Dylan said at the same time. "I'm gonna grab some water. Be right back. You ladies stay put," Dylan said, disappearing down the street and leaving Honor alone with four sets of eyes narrowed on her like they wanted all the details of her sex life.

"Now that he's gone, we need the scoop," Mrs. L said with a wink, "Betty told us what a hottie your boyfriend is."

Honor bit the inside of her cheek. Leave it to the four busiest bodies in White Strand to get her alone first thing in the morning after the best weekend of her life. "He's not my —"

"You should have seen his muscles straining through his wet shirt," Mrs. J. said.

The team nodded like they wished they had.

"He's not my boyfriend. And what are you doing checking out someone young enough to be your grandson?

"I may be *older*, but I'm not dead."

Honor sucked in her bottom lip to keep from laughing.

"He's also very charming," Midge said, ignoring Honor's boyfriend rebuttal and reminding her Bryce had been into the Happy Harpoon several times.

He wasn't a stranger in her town anymore.

"You ladies are impossible. We're just… friends."

"Friends with benefits." Mrs. L. said like she'd just coined the term. The rest of the group grinned. At least *they* were enjoying this.

"It's not like that, either." Could she rewind the morning and take a different route please?

"What is it like?" Midge asked. Her grandmotherly voice was inquisitive and sweet, a combination that usually got her the answers she wanted.

"Umm…"

Shirley's hip hummed and she jumped. "Oh, that's my cell," she announced. She lifted her tutu and retrieved the phone. "It's a text from Frannie. She wants to know what's this she hears about Honor and some hotshot agent with tight buns."

Oh. My. God.

And how did the mayor's wife find out about her and Bryce?

"What are you texting back?" Honor asked, watching Shirley text faster than she did.

"That he's your sex slave."

"*What?*" This was a bad dream and any minute now Honor would wake up and go straight to work. Do not walk down Main Street. Do not stop for coffee. Run in the opposite direction if she ever saw the Street Team again.

Shirley looked up. "Kidding, sweetie."

Midge put her hand on Honor's arm. "We love you. And we're happy you're finally moving on with such a nice young man."

What did that mean? Moving on. No one knew what was inside her head. How could they? "You ladies need to find something else to talk about." She stepped around them and waved an arm over her head. "Something more age appropriate," she added over her shoulder, "like adding fiber to your diets."

"She's definitely in love," Mrs. Landry said, prompting Honor to hurry her steps.

Love? That was crazy talk. And damn it all. She'd be the talk of the town now. Everyone would speculate and whisper and watch her every move. She knew no one meant any harm, but she hated being under a microscope.

Love, she mentally repeated, and her heart did a wheelie. She rubbed a few fingers across her chest to banish the uncool display from the stupid organ.

Instead of going to the mayor's office, she took off in a different direction. Palm trees shaded most of her walk, but by the time she got to her destination tiny beads of sweat trickled down her sides. She knocked on the door. It swung open. "Hi, Uncle Tuck."

He took one look at her and opened his arms. She stayed in the cocoon of his embrace for a good long while before they moved outside to the deck.

Still they didn't talk, just sat in companionable silence and watched the waves roll onto shore in the distance. Like her, Uncle Tuck didn't always need words to fill the space.

"I got a fish."

"Gold?"

"Puffer."

"Even better."

"His name is Jaws."

"No better name than that."

"I'm pretty sure he's worked his way into my heart."

Uncle Tuck turned away from the sea and looked at her. She kept her attention straight ahead so all he saw was her profile. That would be enough for him to figure out she wasn't only talking about a fish.

Her uncle heard things too. He was fooling around with Mrs. L., after all, and that right there meant a front row seat to everything going on in the cove. Honor hadn't been hiding her relationship with Bryce. But they wouldn't be seen together again and how did she explain that? Would people look at her with pity and assume she'd screwed up again?

"Did I ever tell you the story about how I met Veronica?" he said.

"No."

He settled back into his Adirondack chair. "I'd just finished surfing. It was late in the day and most of the other guys had left. I'd parked my car in the bike lane and was changing out of my wetsuit. I had a towel around my waist and nothing else when I closed the driver's side door and my towel got stuck."

Honor twisted to face her uncle and brought her knees up to her chest. She fought a smile.

"When I tried to open the door, it was locked. I looked through the window and my keys were right there on the front seat. I'd locked my goddamn keys in the car and was stuck with nothin' but a towel on."

A little giggle escaped through her pressed lips.

One corner of Tuck's mouth lifted into an impish grin. He never took himself too seriously.

"So a car pulls in behind mine and parks. This knockout

gets out. Long legs, great rack, blond hair. She goes around to her trunk and starts pulling out camera equipment. A tripod, big black canvas case. Then her head peeks around the corner of the car and her eyes lock on mine. 'Need some help?' she says. 'You offering?' I ask back.

"She picks up her stuff and strides over to me, her eyes never leaving mine. They're green and bright and they're laughing. She's laughing at me and right there I knew I was gonna ask this woman to marry me. She tells me she's a photographer. I tell her I'm a surfer. 'Got anything on under there?' she says. 'Nope,' I say. She sizes me up then, says, 'Tell you what, I've got a box full of swimwear in my backseat for shoots. I'll get you a pair of trunks if you model for me with your surfboard.' 'Deal,' I tell her. She smiles and walks around to the passenger side of her car. I follow her."

"Tuck!"

He grinned. "She didn't even flinch. Checked out my junk and told me this was gonna be the start to a beautiful relationship. It was."

Honor cast soft eyes on her great uncle. The man could make her laugh and sigh at the same time. "Do you ever regret walking away?"

"Ah, the "R" word." He ran a hand along his tanned, clean-shaven jaw, his skin creased from all his days spent in the surf and sun, but still handsome as ever. "That word comes back like a pesky fly that won't go away."

"Or like a scent that clings to you no matter how many times you wash your hands." She could still sometimes smell Lance's bodywash and she hated that.

Tuck gave her arm a quick squeeze. "Here's the thing. Walking with our heads down trying to pull the weight of our mistakes doesn't make them go away. Choice is the only thing that conquers regret. Choosing to learn from our past and waking up with hope on the pillowcase beside us rather than remorse."

"I wish there was a magic pill."

"There is. It's called Vi—"

"Stop!" She sent him her sternest, most forbidding glare. He was almost as bad as the Street Team.

He chuckled. "Do I regret not marrying Veronica? Yes and no. She ended up marrying a great guy and they've got a boatload of grandkids. Do I regret all the days I spent with her? No. Hell no. Some of my greatest memories are of the two of us. So you see, there's good wrapped up in things we might regret, too.

"I've learned to wake up with the conviction that I'm better than my past. And you are too, Sunshine."

She blinked back tears. "I can't… I don't…" She'd gotten so used to the idea that she couldn't commit to anything for the long haul that she didn't believe anything else. She and Bryce had said goodbye on good terms. But if there was the possibility of more… "I'll fail him. I know I will."

"I don't see how that's possible. Fish are very simple creatures."

The corners of her mouth lifted up. Tuck smiled in return before he said, "So are men."

Yes, but she wasn't.

Tuck studied her. "I can see your mind working between what if's and what not's and whether or not you deserve to be happy. You do, Sunshine. For a long time now, you've been lost, and here's what I want you to do.

"Find yourself in the present. See the possibilities right in front of you and hold on tight to the ones you want to keep."

She let all his words sink in. She did that already, didn't she? Lived impulsively and for fun. Independent and uninhibited.

"Regret isn't real," Tuck said. "It's something invented to punish ourselves."

*That* hit her like a two hundred pound punching bag. She *was* still punishing herself for what happened with Lance.

"So," he said standing up, and slapping his hands on his thighs. "You eat yet? How about some French toast?"

"Sounds good." She followed him into the kitchen where he shared more stories that centered around his lack of clothing.

And for the first time in a very long while, she didn't feel *all* the weight of her mistakes on her shoulders.

She left Tuck's a little while later for her antique store so she wouldn't have to face Shirley again. The floor shined like new. Danny had put her shelves together. "Pay, it's starting to look really good in here." Her painted wall still looked like it had been brushed with kid fingers instead of bristles, but if she squinted, it didn't look half bad. She plopped down in the middle of the room to soak it all in just as her cell rang.

"Hello?" she said with hesitancy. She didn't recognize the number.

"Hello. Is Honor Mitchell there please?"

"This is she."

"Hi, Honor. My name is Beth Rhodes and I was hoping to hire you. Bryce Bishop gave me your number."

Caught off guard and a little confused, she didn't answer right away.

"I'm sorry," Beth said, "Did I catch you in the middle of something? I'm happy to call back later."

"Uh, no. No." She jumped to her feet and went to her desk. "Now's fine. How do you know Bryce?"

"He represents my husband. He was at the house this morning for a meeting and we got on the topic of antiques since I've been hoping to find a chest from the Victorian era similar to the one my great grandmother had. Bryce mentioned you were the best antique dealer on the west coast."

Honor didn't know what to say. She could barely catch

her breath.

"Hello?"

She scrambled for a pen and paper. "Yes. I'm here. Let me just write down your name and number and if you could email me exactly what you're looking for, I'd be happy to help you out."

"That's wonderful. Thank you."

Beth recited her phone number and Honor shared her email address. She asked for Honor's fee next and Honor spit out the first number to come to mind. A ridiculously high hourly rate she wished she could take back the moment she heard it aloud, but Beth simply said that sounded great.

Wow. Honor put her phone on the desk and brought her hands to her face, covering her mouth and nose in utter surprise and…excitement. She had her first real client thanks to Bryce.

She smiled against her palms. His faith in her made her believe anything was possible.

. . .

One text.

One text thanking him for referring a client to her and his resolve to stay away had crashed and burned. More texts followed. Honor had the power to permanently damage his heart, to ruin his chances with her brother.

And still being careless won out over caution.

How had a one night stand turned into more? He'd told himself to keep his emotions off the table, but that had been impossible the second she'd surrendered under his touch. She made him forget himself.

He'd lasted four days. Every day he'd told himself they were done. And every day his heart begged to differ. He couldn't remember the last time he'd played hooky from work, but when Honor texted him she was feeling under the weather and home alone, he'd decided to surprise her. Illness aside, she inspired spontaneity in him and he liked it.

He parked in front of her house and headed straight for the fake rock he'd noticed in the planter near her front door. A shiny silver key revealed itself when he slid the rock open.

Quiet filled the house so he walked down the hallway to Honor's bedroom and knocked lightly. When she didn't answer, he went inside. The covers were up to her chin, her hands tucked under the side of her beautiful face. He sat on the edge of the bed and watched her sleep. He'd never tire of staring at her.

She must have sensed his presence because she rolled onto her back and stretched her arms. Her eyelids fluttered open and when she finally focused on him, her pink lips curved into a sexy morning smile that got an immediate rise out of him.

"Hi," she said, her voice a little rough with sleep.

"Morning."

Then she blinked herself wide-awake and bolted upright. The comforter slipped to her waist, revealing a low V-cut nightgown with thin straps. He'd wanted to kiss her lips. Now he wanted to kiss the freckle above her left breast. Her neck. Her shoulder. Everywhere.

"I thought I was dreaming. What are you doing here?"

"Thought I'd surprise you. Make sure you were okay."

She twisted her hands in her lap. "You could have just called."

"I needed to see for myself how sick you are."

She covered her mouth and gave a tiny cough. "It's nothing serious. You really didn't have to drive all the way here."

"But since I did, how about getting some fresh air with me?" He stood. "Get dressed and I'll wait in the living room."

A swallow worked its way down her throat. They hadn't talked about what keeping in touch meant, but he wasn't ready to give her up. Last weekend, she'd let all her barriers down and he'd never felt more connected to another person. He wanted that again.

She sighed deeply. "I don't know if that's such a good idea."

"You haven't heard what I have planned yet," he pointed out.

"What do you have planned?"

"It's a surprise." *You like surprises, remember.* He remembered every word she'd said to him. "I promise it'll be fun."

"And if it's not?" She twirled her finger around the hair falling over her shoulder. "Fun, I mean."

"You're looking at the King of Fun."

That put a twinkle in her eyes. "King, huh? What if I decide you're only a prince?"

"Then I'll make you my princess instead of my queen."

She rolled her eyes, but laughed. "That is so cheesy."

God, her laugh did scary good things to him. "There's plenty more where that came from. So?"

She waved him off. "I'll be out in ten."

"Make it nine. I'm pretty sure I can't wait ten to see you again." He turned and left the room, even though a big part of him wanted to join her in bed instead. While he waited for Honor to dress, he spent a few minutes with Jaws and then noticed a postcard from Hallmark wishing her a happy birthday with a discount. He picked it up.

"What are doing?" she asked from behind him.

Bryce put the piece of mail down. "Wondering when your birthday is." He turned and animal-style lust shot through his veins. "Wow. You look amazing."

"Thanks." She ran her hands down the short, sleeveless

coral print dress that hugged her curves. "I wasn't sure what we were doing, but it looks beautiful out today. I'm ready for whatever the King of Fun has up his sleeve."

He closed the distance between them, cupped her cheek with one hand, her nape with the other, and stared at the tiny flecks of silver in her eyes. She tunneled her fingers through his hair and pulled him in for a kiss.

A deep, long, slow kiss that promised they'd come back to this later. Thank God they were on the same wavelength.

"So," he murmured against her lips. "Birthday?"

She slowly pulled back. "April first." He raised an eyebrow. "Yes, April Fool's Day. And yes, jokes are played on me left and right. When's yours?"

"July seventeenth."

"A summer boy."

"Yep. So come on, Spring Girl, let's go have some fun." He took her hand and led her to his car. Mrs. Jamison stood in her front yard watering flowers and waved. Bryce waved back just as she whipped her cell phone out of her pocket.

Before putting the car in drive, he took his own cell out to check directions for their short drive.

"You figuring out my surprise?" she asked, trying to peek at his screen.

He dropped the phone into the driver's door pocket. "Not anymore." Twenty minutes later he parked in a dirt lot with only a few other cars and they walked toward the butterfly pavilion tucked away in the mountains. Even from a distance he could see the shadows of tiny winged creatures in action. Honor slipped her hand inside his and practically skipped to the entrance.

The fastening of their fingers seemed very date-like, but he pushed the idea away. Today was about fun. He didn't want to think too hard about what they were doing, just enjoy Honor's company.

"I've heard about this place and was hoping to get up here."

"It's like I can read your mind," he teased.

She cast him a flirty glance. "Tell me what I'm thinking right now and I'll tell you what I have on under this dress."

Hell. She wanted him to speak when all he could do now was picture her body sans the dress?

"Problem?" She prompted, making fun of his silence.

He glanced at his wrist. "Actually my watch tells me you're not wearing anything."

"Sorry Charlie, but I am."

"Damn," he shook his arm. "It must be fast."

Honor snickered. "Now that is the cheesiest line ever. And I've heard a lot of lines."

"Any of them ever work?" They got to the entrance of the exhibit and Bryce paid the entry fee.

"You fishing for the 4-1-1 on my past love life?"

He put his arm around her waist as he pushed open the door to the pavilion. "I'll tell you about mine if you tell me about yours."

"This is butterfly heaven," Honor said instead of answering his question. Greenery filled the glass-enclosed building and butterflies collected everywhere. Hundreds of them. A huge grin spread across her face as she watched the tiny winged creatures.

"Looks like," he said.

They followed the winding cobblestone path before them with slow measured steps. The warm, humid air left water droplets clinging to most of the leaves on the plants.

Honor put her finger out next to a leaf like she hoped the butterfly there would climb aboard. Its turquoise blue and brown wings were stationary, but then it moved a little to the right and tickled her skin. She bounced up and down with excitement and the butterfly quickly flew away.

"You must keep very, very still, Padawan," Bryce said.

Honor whipped around to find a butterfly on his shoulder, his finger, and his arm. "You're a Star Wars fan?"

"Who isn't?" His grin widened. "Now don't move. There's a red and yellow butterfly in your hair. And another about to land on your shoulder."

Super slowly, she dropped her chin and darted her eyes to her left. The tiny creature had orange wings with black trim and white polka dots. "Hey there," she murmured without moving her lips.

Bryce watched her in fascination before breaking his butterfly connection and saying, "Come on. I think I see a butterfly orgy going on and they'll definitely want you involved."

"I don't know. You were the first one to get some action." She followed his lead, her little friends fluttering away. "A guy who smells as good as you obviously attracts attention."

He stopped and brought her flush against him. "I could breathe you in all day, Honor. You're like sunshine in a bottle and I can't get enough of you."

She touched her nose to his. "I'm kind of stuck on you, too."

"I didn't mean for this happen," he admitted.

"I didn't either."

And then like some enchantment had been cast over them, butterflies by the bunch flew in circles around them. He and Honor kept perfectly still, eyes locked on one another, until the free flying creatures moved elsewhere and broke the spell.

"That was awesome," she said.

Happy he'd been the guy to bring her awesome, Bryce grinned and took her hand. They explored further, discovering furry caterpillars, more spectacularly colorful species of butterflies, and plant life that blossomed the most unique flowers.

Once they'd walked the whole cobblestone path, they settled on a concrete bench. Honor sighed with pleasure and leaned against his side.

"I've only had one boyfriend," she whispered. "A long time ago."

Every time she shared another piece of herself Bryce wanted to pump his fists in the air. And foolish or not, he cared more deeply with each revelation. "How long ago?"

"High school."

Bryce turned his head, but she kept her gaze forward. "What happened?"

"He wanted forever and I freaked out. I stood him up for his senior prom and the next day he…" She coughed into the bend of her arm before a swallow visibly made its way down her throat. "The next day he tried to kill himself."

"Oh, sweetheart." Bryce wrapped her in his arms, cupping the back of her head with his hand. "I'm sorry he did that to you."

"I did it to him," she said, her face in the crux of his neck.

"No you didn't. He did it to himself. To break *you*."

He felt her blink against the skin above his shirt collar. "Lance did break me and you're the first person to recognize it."

Jesus. How had no one realized that? No one deserved retaliation like Honor had suffered. No wonder she didn't want another relationship. She not only had doubts about herself, but about putting her certainty in another person.

Which made him the last guy she should be with. He was still waiting on Cooper's decision. Still keeping a hold on his heart, not sure he had it in him to let someone in again. The man Honor learned to trust should be in it for the long haul.

Not someone who could do her wrong because he didn't know what his priorities were anymore.

# Chapter Eleven

Honor's entire body quivered. Bryce messed with all her practiced habits big time—had from the very beginning. Maybe she could trust herself to be with someone again. Maybe, like her favorite movie touted, "people do belong to each other, because that's the only chance anybody's got for real happiness." It felt right with Bryce.

That thought-bomb, though, needed some getting used to. She hopped to her feet. "I'm hungry. You hungry?"

He stood. "I am and I know just the place."

"What if I know just the place?" She put a little extra swing in her step as he followed behind her.

"There's no way it's as good as mine."

"Oh, really?" She loved getting back to the playful banter between them. He lifted the fragile memories she hated to let inside her head and kept her rooted in the present.

"Hands down, you'll love this joint." He held the pavilion door open for her.

The sun rested high in the sky and a warm breeze brushed over her skin. She brought a hand to her forehead to shield her eyes from the brightness. "And if I don't, promise to do whatever I say with those hands of yours?"

He put said delicious hands on her hips and bent his head so his mouth grazed that sensitive spot just under her earlobe. "I'll do whatever you want."

She shivered. "I guess we'll go to your place then."

"Damn right."

He made sure she got in the car okay and then hurried around to his side. His polite gestures quirked up the corners of her mouth every single time. She loved that he was a gentleman out in public, but dirty in the bedroom.

Fifteen minutes later they arrived at a food truck parked at the beach along the coast highway. FRENCH FRY HEAVEN was stamped on the side in big gold letters with a halo around 'Fry.' A ton of people stood in line.

Bryce handed her a blanket he pulled from his trunk. "Find a spot on the sand and I'll grab us the best fries you've ever eaten."

"We'll see about that." Although given the crowd, she felt pretty sure they would be. "And by the way, this isn't a joint."

He rolled his eyes. "It's an establishment where food is served."

"Or it's a truck." She smirked and made her way toward the water.

Lying back on her elbows, her feet digging in the sand, she watched the waves push onto shore. A little boy scrambled to keep his feet dry, running forward and back, giggling with his mom close by his side. Honor had played the same game as a young girl.

"Close your eyes," Bryce said, his shadow falling over her.

She did as he asked, a wave of excitement and anticipation sweeping from her fingers to her toes. The blanket rustled. She almost peeked at him, her curiosity getting the best of her, but the element of surprise kept her lids closed.

The first thing to hit her senses was the smell of delicious fried potato and something else—something sweet, but she couldn't pinpoint what exactly.

"It smells yummy," she said.

Bryce's arm brushed hers, setting off the usual flurry of tingles when they touched. He sat close. Super close. She wanted to roll over on top of him and line their bodies up so that she could nibble her way down a French fry he held in his teeth. Kiss. Swallow. Repeat.

"This isn't an ordinary French fry," he said, his husky voice making her even tinglier.

She pushed up off her elbows and tucked her arms underneath her legs. The sunshine and the ridiculously hot and adorable man next to her were a killer combination, and she needed a more fixed position before she melted into the sand. "No?"

He feathered his lips over her jaw, scooted closer so she could rest against him. "Would I give the most interesting woman I know a regular fry? I don't think so."

"You just gonna talk or feed me?"

"You like the way I talk."

"Not really," she lied. Would he get on with the French fries already?

"Your body says otherwise." And he proved it by brushing his hand across her breast and feeling her nipple strain to reach him.

She sucked in a breath. The brush had been quick, but just feeling his nearness had her pressing her thighs together. "This needs to stay G-rated, Mr. Bishop. We are on a public beach."

"Right," he said, as if the reminder supremely disappointed him. "So this particular French fry is known as a waffle fry." Something warm—the edge of the fry, she guessed—touched her lip for a brief second. "Or *pommes gaufrette* for you word connoisseurs."

"Also known as crisscross fries," she offered, breathing in the delicious scent. With her eyes closed, the smell came across stronger.

"That's right." The waffle fry touched her mouth again, but when she parted her lips, he pulled it away, the big tease.

She licked her bottom lip. He groaned. Warmth, want, need, desire, all swept over her.

She'd never forget this simple act of being fed a French fry.

"What makes this better than other waffle fries is that it's dusted with something special. Ready to see if you can guess what that is?"

"Yes."

"Damn, you are so sexy, Honor." His warm breath fanned over her jaw. "I want to feed you my mouth and nothing else."

"*Nothing* else?" She leaned closer, her side softening against his chest.

"Okay, one other thing, but we'll get to that later. Open up, beautiful." He put the fry in her mouth and she took a bite.

"Mmm. Gimme more."

He fed her the rest of the crispy fried potato and then two more.

"What do you think?" he said.

"I think I've died and gone to heaven."

"Hence the name of the truck."

"And I think the mystery flavor is Nesquick. Can I open my eyes now?"

He laughed. "Yes."

It took a minute for her eyes to adjust to the brightness, tiny white dots dancing in front of her before she focused on the handsome man beside her. "There you are," she said, thinking she'd like to open her eyes to see him every day.

"Want another?"

"Yes, please."

Their eyes never left each other as he fed her another fry. This time when he pulled his hand away, she grabbed his wrist so she could lick the tips of his fingers.

The hazel ring around his pupils glittered with lust. "Is that G-rated, Ms. Mitchell?"

"Feeling a little hot under the…belt buckle, Mr. Bishop?" She let go, gave him her best flirty smile.

"Hard, Ms. Mitchell." He bent his head and took her earlobe between his teeth. "I'm feeling hard and you're going to pay for that."

"I can't wait." She broke eye contact and reached for the white paper bag. "Should we hurry and finish these amazing *pommes gaufrettes*?"

"We should. By the way, the dusting," he nodded at the fry in her hand, "is cocoa powder so good guess Smarty Pants." He grabbed his own fry out of the bag and popped it into his mouth.

"I never would've thought to combine the two."

"Surprise."

"You are the King of Surprises." He'd caught her off guard in the best, most wonderful ways. What would it be like to be surprised by him next week? Next month? She blinked away the thought.

"And fun?" He traced his finger down her arm.

"That, too." She'd never experienced this much joy and happiness. Panic boiled over inside her at the magnitude of it. She turned her attention to the water, worried he'd see all the admiration—and fear—on her face.

"Honor?"

"Yes?"

"Let's get out of here."

She could do that. "And get naked again?"

"I think we both know last weekend wasn't enough. We

can try and ignore this pull between us, but maybe it would be better to make some new rules instead. Or better yet, fly by the seat of our pants."

His words, as usual, were like magic. She knew how to fly. How to be spontaneous and not think too far ahead.

She jumped to her feet. "Last one to the car is a rotten egg."

He drove like a NASCAR driver back to her place, and ushered her inside so fast there was no way Mrs. Jamison and her spying eyes could have seen them.

Bryce's hands were all over her as they stumbled into her bedroom. He kicked the door shut. Mouths busy, fingers searching, they had each other naked in less than ten seconds.

Honor took him in her hand, stroked him, then dropped to her knees to take him inside her mouth. His hands went to her hair, holding her head in place.

"Yes, just like that," he groaned.

She loved the effect she had on him. Loved feeling him lose control and hearing him gulp for air. She licked him, sucked him, used her hand and mouth until he gripped her shoulders and pulled her to her feet.

"Bed. Now," he said.

They'd made love several times now. Rushed and rowdy. Slow and steady. Careful and mindless. But this time, this time was different.

Because she was different. This wasn't a one-night thing for either of them anymore. And with every kiss and heady surge of his hips, she felt like he was branding her, opening her eyes and mind to a new point of view. Fear she'd mess up this beautiful thing lingered, but stronger was the desire to open herself up. To follow her heart, to give her heart, and see what Bryce did with it. She'd rather he hurt her than the other way around.

He stared down at her with intensity and unabashed

affection and she wrapped her legs tighter around his waist, dug her nails deeper into his lower back. Their sweat-slicked bodies moved together in impossibly perfect tempo. When she exploded with soul-shattering spasms, he continued to hold her snug in his arms until her breathing slowed. Then he brought her knees up higher and rocked inside her with white-hot strokes that made her moan and gasp and took her right back to that beautiful edge of release.

She brought one arm up to thread her fingers through his hair before cupping his head and bringing his lips to hers. He devoured her mouth until she cried out another release with fearless abandon. A few moments later his magnificent body shuddered and his husky groan of satisfaction filled the room.

They lay tangled in each other until sleep came, the last thought in her head how much she loved and appreciated that he made her forget.

But forgetting about her mistakes didn't mean forgiving herself for them and until she did that, she'd never be able to move forward.

• • •

Honor's antique shop looked great compared to the last time Bryce had seen it. Items sat on shelves, small pieces of furniture were shined and placed, and the wall Honor told him not to pay attention to didn't—

"I said not to look at it!" She practically tackled him from behind, putting her hands on his upper arms and turning his body toward the windows. "If you can't follow one simple direction then you're going to have to leave."

He spun around before she could step away and attacked her mouth with his. She hesitated only a second before giving back with equal energy, her hands in his hair. She liked messing up his hair. He smiled against her mouth.

"What?" she asked, pulling back.

"Nothing." He skimmed her bottom lip with the pad of his thumb. "Just that I like kissing you. Maybe we should christen this place?" He waggled his eyebrows.

"You're insatiable."

"Can't help it." He'd proven that to her all afternoon.

She fell against his chest, looped her arms loosely around his neck. "Can you resist me long enough for me to check my email and do a few other little things?"

"If I have to." He slid his hands down her back to her very fine ass. He fought the temptation to lift her dress and cop a better feel.

"Thank you." She moved to her desk and fired up her computer.

"Danny did a great job on your floors." He wandered around the small shop, avoiding direct eye contact with the purple wall of shame. It didn't look *that* bad.

"He did. Did you know he fixed Mrs. Jamison's gate?"

"I mentioned the gate needed some repair but I didn't know he'd helped already."

Honor shuffled some papers on her desk. "Yes, and then Mrs. J. referred him to Shirley because her fence was coming down or something, and he fixed that, too. Word has it he's also helped a few other people. Sophie and I were in the Beach Café the other morning and she mentioned he does all sorts of woodwork, including making furniture." She glanced up with a pained expression on her face. "Now the Street Team is talking about Danny's wood."

"Street Team?"

"Don't ask." She waved off his question and went back to her computer.

Bryce knew Danny had been in White Strand more often lately to help Zane with some tax stuff, but he hadn't realized he'd become so popular.

"So, um, I have to write up an invoice for Beth Rhodes and that means I need to actually have a name for this place."

He inwardly smiled. Beth had been the unintentional catalyst that brought him back to Honor.

"What do you think of the name Driftwood?" she asked. "When we were little Payton and I used to collect pieces and build beach houses for our Barbie dolls." She sat back in her chair with a faraway look in her eyes. "I also like it because I picture beaches all over the world with driftwood and how it sort of connects us all. It could come from anywhere, just like the antiques I want to find and sell."

"I think it's a great name." He stopped in front of her desk.

"Really?" She blinked up at him and he hoped she saw how proud he was of her.

"It's a keeper."

The grin she flashed before going back to her computer put him over the moon. Seeing her happy drove every other thought but her out of his head. For a long time work had meant more to him than anything else, but when he was with Honor he didn't think about business. Had he let his client list interfere with his personal relationships in the past? Maybe.

He had no idea where things would lead with Honor, and contradictory emotions still sat in the back of his mind. But if ever there was a risk worth taking again… was it with her? Could she heal his blackened heart? Could he heal hers?

"You busy next Saturday night?" he asked.

Her fingers kept tapping away on the keyboard. "I don't think so."

"I'm being honored at a charity dinner and would like for you to go with me."

She froze, like time stood still and Bryce was the only one breathing. When she finally raised her eyes to his, he didn't know what to make of her blank expression.

"You mean as your date?" she said quietly.

"Yes."

"You want me to be with you when you receive an award." Not a question, more like a crazy fact she couldn't wrap her head around.

"Yes," he answered with conviction. Until he heard from Cooper, he saw no reason not to keep seeing Honor. Once he got a yes or no answer from the skateboarder, he'd figure out what to do then.

Her gaze fell to her desk. "Will your family be there?"

"Yes. And so will Danny, Zane and Sophie. Look at it as an excuse to dress up and have a night out."

"This is a big deal."

"The evening or the date?" He couldn't be sure, but he had a feeling if he handed her a brown paper bag, she'd be grateful to breathe into it.

She let out a sigh. "Both."

"The dinner is an annual event put on by the Bishop Foundation to recognize contributions by volunteers and people in the community. My grandmother started the organization to honor my grandfather and its grown quite a bit since then. In the past it's been a relatively small celebration. Maybe a hundred and fifty people. Having you as my date will make me the envy of every man in the room. But more importantly," he lifted her hand off the desk and rubbed his thumb across her knuckles. "When you're near me I'm infinitely happier."

She lifted her eyes back to his. "You don't play fair."

"I only speak the truth."

"At the precise moment to catch a girl at her weakest."

He frowned. There was nothing weak about her.

She pulled her hand back and rolled her eyes. "How can I say no when you've spent the past four hours making *me* infinitely happier by giving me orgasm after orgasm and all I can think about is you doing it again."

"So that's a yes?" He flashed her a roguish smile.

"Plus you took me to see butterflies." She fell back against her chair in happy defeat, the dreamy expression on her face giving her away.

"And don't forget spoke French to you."

His reminder provoked a sexy grin to take hold of lips still swollen from his kisses. They stayed latched to each other's gaze until she broke eye contact and said, "I don't know how to do this, Bryce."

"Sure you do. Just be yourself. I've never met anyone who puts others at ease as quickly as you do and you might pretend you don't like to be social, but I know you secretly want to dress up and paint the town. No one wears a dress like you do."

She shook her head in mock discomfort, the slight turn at the corners of her mouth sharing her true disposition. "Is this a formal dinner?"

"Yes. I'll be in a tux."

Silence dragged on for what seemed like hours before she finally blessed him with an agreeable smile. "Okay, I'll be your date. But only because you probably look obscenely hot in a tux."

"Of course."

"And Sophie needs a gal pal," Honor said.

"I think Olivia is going to be there, too. You remember her from the wedding?"

"I do." Honor's shoulder's visibly relaxed. "So you'll have several friends there."

If it made her feel better to be lumped in with his friends, so be it. As long as she was at the event, he didn't care what kind of rationalization she used.

"Hello?"

Honor quickly turned her head at the sound of a female

voice coming from the open doorway of the store. She jumped to her feet, almost knocking over her chair. "Mary?"

The older woman smiled. "Surprise."

"Oh my gosh." Honor rushed into the woman's open arms. They held each other for a long time. Long enough for Bryce to feel like an intruder.

"I've missed you," Mary said, pulling back. She regarded Honor with big brown eyes filled with motherly love.

Bryce sucked in a breath. He'd never met Mary, but staring at her face he knew who she was. Over Honor's shoulder, her gaze connected with his.

Honor twisted around and when their eyes met, pain spoiled the blue he'd come to adore. Tension so thick filled the space between them, the only way to end it would be to leave. Suddenly, he'd give anything to have an ocean between them.

"I should head out," he said.

"Okay. But uh, before you go, I'd like you to meet Payton's mom, Mary. Mary, this is… this is my friend Bryce." Mary looked between them. Honor never broke eye contact with him. "Payton's Bryce."

His gut clenched. Did she still think that? After everything that had happened between them? "It's nice to meet you," he said.

"Likewise." Mary shook his outstretched hand, her expression warm, but also sympathetic.

He had to get out of there before he suffocated. Honor's loyalty would always lay with her best friend, and where that left him he didn't know. But he certainly didn't want anyone's pity.

"Have a nice visit," he said before he forced a smile and walked out of the store without a glance back.

• • •

Honor watched Bryce leave and guilt chewed up her insides all over again. She wasn't sure what she'd done wrong, but hurt had been written all over his face and she hated herself for putting it there. *That's what you do, you bring pain.*

"That was him, huh?" Mary said.

"Yes."

"There's something going—"

"Yes."

"Want to talk about it?"

"No."

Mary took her hand and led her to the window seat. "It's okay, you know." Honor kept her eyes on their entwined hands. It wasn't okay. None of this was okay. "Sometimes what's meant to be happens from loss."

Honor lifted her head. "You really think so?"

"I do. And I'll tell you why. This store for one." Mary scanned the space. "It's coming along beautifully."

"Thanks. I've named it Driftwood."

"That's a fabulous name. I remember you and Payton making huts with it when you were little."

"Uh-huh."

"She's looking down on you, you know. With a smile and appreciation for keeping her in your thoughts."

"I think about her every day," Honor said softly. "How have you been?"

"Every day gets easier." Mary glanced down, gave Honor's hand a squeeze and then let go. "You got the tattoo."

Honor rubbed her finger across the ink. The way Mary said, *the tattoo*, raised goose bumps on Honor's skin. "Yes?"

Mary chuckled. "You always wanted one. You don't remember? It was Ally's Sweet Sixteen, I think, and you and Payton got Henna tattoos. Pay hated hers, but you loved yours and told your mother that you were going to get a real tattoo before you turned twenty-five."

A rush of memories flooded Honor. She'd forgotten all about that. "And Mom said she'd go with me if I was worried about the needle." She thought about Bryce and how he'd been there for her with his supportive touch and playful word game.

"I guess you did okay."

More than okay. Honor gave a small nod.

"Have you crossed everything off your list?"

Honor froze. "*What?*"

Mary took a deep breath. "I'm here to make a confession. The list Payton wrote was for you."

"I don't understand." Honor stood and wrapped her arms around herself. Mary knew about the list?

"I don't know everything Pay put on it because she wanted to keep some things private, but the list wasn't about her like she told you. She made me promise to come see you before your birthday and tell you that."

The temperature in the room shot up a hundred degrees, and quite possibly the walls were actually closing in. "What are you saying?"

Mary got to her feet. "Payton was dying and she wanted you to live, Honor. She'd watched you close yourself off since breaking up with Lance and she hoped this would be a way for you to reclaim some of your old self. She wanted you to rediscover you could see things through. You've always deserved success, Honor, you just wouldn't let yourself believe it."

Mary put her hand on Honor's arm. "And she knew you wouldn't do it for yourself. But that you'd do it for her. So she fibbed a little."

Honor stumbled back, her head a massive jumble of emotions. "She lied to me?"

"Because she loved you."

That was true. And she knew Honor better than she knew

herself. Maybe it took a lie to make a person find what they were capable of. Honor did feel more accomplished since crossing things off Pay's list. A mixture of relief and courage ran through Honor's veins.

This was all on her now and it felt strangely... good.

# Chapter Twelve

Honor got home Wednesday night and collapsed onto her couch. She'd worked nonstop the past five days, spending all day locked away at the mayor's office and then her off-hours at Driftwood. Decorating and furnishing the store was the easy and fun part. But things like licenses and insurance and something called a DBA were beyond her scope of understanding. So when Danny had stopped in earlier today, she hadn't questioned what he was doing there. She just asked for help and he gave it.

She let out a deep, satisfied breath. Payton would be proud of her.

The doorbell rang, but unwilling to move from her comfy spot, she didn't budge. "Come in," she called out.

"It's not too early for the Boogeyman, you know."

Honor jolted up at the sound of Bryce's voice. They hadn't spoken since he'd left Driftwood the day Mary visited and by the ill humor in his voice, he wasn't exactly happy to see her now. "Umm…"

"Are you home alone?"

"Yes." Was that good? Bad? Was he supposed to meet up with Cooper?

"Then you really should keep your door locked." His unfriendly tone irked her.

"And ruin visits from the Boogeyman?" she teased, because he might be in a bad mood, but she wasn't.

He shook his head and took the spot next to her on the couch. "Danny and I had dinner with Zane and afterwards, I somehow ended up here. Weird, huh?" Finally, like he couldn't fight it anymore, the corners of his mouth lifted. The slight crack of a sexy mischievous smile combined with that chin and those cheeks and those eyes, turned her to mush.

"Very." She scooted closer, took his arm and put it around her. Now she wasn't just mush. She was mushy mush. He smelled super good.

"You're like a homing device whenever I get within a certain range."

She laughed. "So long as you don't start calling me Pigeon, we're good. Hey," she picked up his hand. "I see you got your stitches removed. I'm glad you remembered to do that."

"The nurse said you did good."

She looked up at him. "I'm, uh, also glad you stopped by. Is everything okay?" His clothes were a little more rumpled than normal, his hair not as neat as usual.

"Yeah. Just some stuff going on with work."

"Is that it?" She'd replayed the last words they'd spoken over and over again and kept thinking somehow she'd messed up. *You called him Payton's Bryce.*

"I have to tell you something," she rushed out before he could answer. She brought her knee up and turned to face him. Even weary and wrinkled he looked sexy. Her stomach fluttered. "Two things actually. First, I'm sorry if I hurt you when I introduced you to Mary. That wasn't my intention."

"I haven't been Payton's for a long time, Honor, and

honestly, looking back, I never really was."

Honor nodded and swallowed the lump in her throat. "And second, Payton's list was meant for me."

He sat taller, his eyes twinkled, like she'd just given him a gift. "Go on."

She did. She told him everything about her conversation with Mary. He listened, asked a few questions, and said he appreciated her apology.

"So whatever happens now is what you want to happen."

"Yes." She liked being back in control.

"How does that feel?" He laid his arm across the top of the couch and played with a strand of hair at her shoulder.

"Good."

"And you and me?" He inched closer, the sparkle in his eyes telling her he knew full well what his nearness did to her.

"I think there will always be some small pang of guilt over Payton, but I don't think she'd want us to shy away from each other because of it."

"I agree. So we're still on for Saturday?"

"I hope so."

"Absolutely." He inched closer still. "Unfortunately, I've got to meet with a client in the afternoon, which means I won't have enough time to come pick you up before the dinner. Would you mind catching a ride with Zane and Sophie and meeting me there?"

"Not at all."

"You could stay at my place after."

"I'd like that." She'd missed him. Plain and simple.

He leaned over and kissed her. It started too tentative for her liking so she palmed the back of his head and deepened the kiss. His tongue played with hers while he shifted them with an arm around her waist until she was on her back and he was on top of her. She loved the way he kissed her, like she was essential to his well being.

It was becoming more and more clear that he was essential to hers.

The very loud and very inconvenient growl of her stomach broke them apart. He gazed down at her. "When was the last time you ate?"

She scrunched up her nose. "This morning. I've been busy."

"Come on." He pulled her to feet and led her to the kitchen. "I'll make you my famous bowl of cereal. Sit."

Honor watched him grab a bowl and spoon and put it down on the table in front of her. He opened the cupboard next and contemplated the selection before picking Cocoa Krispies. Her favorite. He poured the cereal into her bowl then grabbed the milk out of the fridge. "What makes this famous, you ask? The perfect amount of milk—added to give the perfect ratio of cereal to milk so there is nothing but an empty bowl when you're finished."

Honor dug right in as Bryce took the chair next to her. "Friday night Zane and Sophie wanted to know if we'd like to go out to dinner with them," he said.

"A double date?" she asked with her mouth full.

"I think you said double date and not bubble gate so I'm going to say yes."

She almost spewed her food at him. He said the best things. "I guess that's okay," she said around the next bite.

Bryce put his chin in his hand and stared at her with a dreamy look.

"Stop."

"Spop?"

Who knew she could smile and chew at the same time? And several happy bites later she discovered Bryce did indeed have magical cereal powers. She dropped her spoon with a clink into the empty bowl.

"Can you do it again?" She never ate just one bowl of

cereal. Sometimes she even ate three, not that she would tonight in front of Bryce.

"You bet I can."

Once again, Honor ate and finished with equal parts cereal and milk. Her guy had talent. Twenty minutes later tangled in the sheets on her bed she finished with Bryce deep inside her and his name on her lips.

Really excellent talent.



"Have I told you how fantastic you look?" Bryce whispered, his mouth taking a little tour behind her earlobe as they sat at a table waiting for Zane and Sophie on Friday night. Sophie had chosen the Italian restaurant just outside White Strand claiming a craving for pasta with scallops.

Honor craved privacy, so it was perfect. The White Strand rumor mill had her practically engaged to Bryce and the less they were seen together in public, the better. Not only was the deceptively sweet sixty-something club texting updates to each other, but Mrs. Jamison had not so secretly taken a photo of her and Bryce as they'd left her house tonight.

Then she'd smiled like she'd just snapped the cover shot for People magazine. Seriously, these ladies needed something better to do.

"Yes, you have." Honor lifted her shoulder and dipped her head to nudge him away, a ticklish giggle escaping her lips. "Now stop."

"Mommy, what is that man doing?"

Bryce must have suspected 'that man' meant him because he pulled back. Sure enough at the table next to them a little girl sat swallowed in the big wooden chair with her eyes on him. He mouthed 'sorry' to the mom. She gave a tiny smile before turning her attention back to the infant in a car seat.

Her husband had his attention on another infant in a car seat. And holy family of six, a little boy stood on his big wooden chair, about to tip the seat over until Dad shot his arm out and settled the boy back down.

Bryce waved to the little girl. She waved back.

"Twins. Twice," the mom said.

"It's our anniversary and we thought we'd give this a try," the dad said.

"Happy anniversary," she and Bryce said in unison. "Oh my Lord," Honor whispered. "Could you even imagine?"

Bryce didn't answer. He was smiling at the little girl now and she was smiling back. Adorable with a capital A.

"Hi guys!" Sophie said with Zane in tow.

"Glad you could join us," Zane added as the newlyweds sat down across the table.

A second later a spitball nailed Zane in the cheek. He swiped his hand across the side of his face and turned to the culprit. "Good shot, bud."

The little boy grinned.

"Oh my god. I'm so sorry," the mom said. "Nicholas, you apologize right now."

"Sowwy."

"No problem," Zane said. Then he put his arm around Sophie and brought her close. "You ready for that?"

Sophie glowed when she looked up at him. "So ready."

Honor's eyes widened. "Is there something you need to tell us?"

Sophie and Zane broke out huge smiles. "We're having a baby," Sophie gushed.

"Congratulations," Bryce said. He reached across the table to shake Zane's hand.

"Thanks, man." A hint of worry flashed in Zane's eyes and Honor guessed it was because of the relationship Zane had had with his own father. A father who had verbally abused his son until he'd passed away. But the way Zane loved Sophie and the way he interacted with kids—who were his biggest fans—left no doubt in Honor's mind he'd be an awesome father.

"Soph!" Honor jumped up and went around to hug her friend. Zane got one, too. "Huge congratulations. I'm so excited for you."

Bryce leaned across the table and kissed Sophie on the cheek. "Congratulations."

"How are you feeling?" Honor asked, settling back in her chair.

"Some days good. Some days not so good."

"Well, you look amazing."

"More gorgeous every day," Zane said, putting his hand on Sophie's flat stomach. "I can't wait to watch you grow."

Wow. Sophie a mom. The waiter stopped to take their drink orders and conversation turned to other things until a loud crash stopped them. Broken plates and glasses scattered across the floor. "I'm so sorry. Is everyone okay?" A waitress asked the family of six.

The babies started bawling.

The little girl started crying and crawled into her mom's lap.

The little boy was about to climb down from his chair to investigate the mess. "Stay put," the dad said.

The babies grew louder, crying at decibels to break the sound barrier.

"Nicholas, I said—" The dad nabbed him just before his little—bare—feet hit the floor. Spiderman sandals sat under his seat.

"Here, let us help," Sophie said, elbowing Zane before standing and hurrying over to the mom. "I can hold the baby if you want, since your arms are full."

"Thank you," the mom said appreciatively. Sophie lifted

the baby out of the car seat.

Zane got up and went to the other car seat. "I can get this one." He studied the carrier for a moment. "I think."

"That'd be great," the dad said with relief. He reached to grab his son's sandals while trying to keep the squirming toddler in his lap.

The wait staff got busy cleaning up and the manager came over to check on everyone and give further apology.

"Oh no," Sophie said, turning white as a ghost and bringing one hand to her mouth with a still crying baby in her arm. Honor jumped to her feet to help, but Bryce beat her to it.

"Here," he said, taking the baby. The careful transfer did funny things to Honor's stomach. "I got it."

"Thank you." And then she took off toward the restroom Honor guessed.

Watching Bryce and Zane bounce and sway from side to side to try and quiet down unhappy babies was quite a sight. "Is there a secret to getting her to stop?" Bryce asked.

"Walk around the table," the mom suggested, trying to pry her daughter's body off of her. "It's okay, sweetie. Let's get you back in your seat so I can hold your sister."

Bryce started to walk, bumped into Zane, and Honor had to stifle a laugh at the terror on their faces, like the slight jolt might hurt the babies.

The baby stopped crying the moment Bryce finished a lap around the table. The other baby had quieted, too, but Honor couldn't take her eyes off the tiny little bundle cradled in Bryce's strong arms. His sleeves were pushed up as usual, and Honor stood there mesmerized by this new human being secure and protected in his hold.

Yellow footed jammies fit over the baby's body. Dark hair covered her perfectly rounded head. Something so small held by something so... good.

A shiver slid down her back.

She looked up to find Bryce's eyes on her. The way those incredible chocolate mocha pools sparkled confirmed what she suspected. He was made to settle down and have a family. Have the white picket fence just like Payton had wanted.

That childhood kissing song, "First comes love, then comes marriage, then comes a baby in a baby carriage," started playing on repeat in her head and she couldn't turn it off. Her heart pounded in her ears for extra effect.

But as things calmed down and the babies went back to their parents and Sophie returned from the restroom, Honor tried to keep herself in the present. She tried not to think ahead and not to think back.

And failed.

"Hey," Bryce whispered. "You okay? You're awfully quiet."

"Just tired," she lied. She wasn't okay at all.

• • •

Bryce worked the ballroom at the Loews Hotel, shaking hands and talking with the guests gathered for the Bishop Foundation's annual dinner to recognize the charity's contributions and the people who had helped make a difference. Tonight he was one of those people, but he really could do without the acknowledgment.

His grandmother had started the foundation when his grandfather passed away. And no one let Ruth Bishop down, least of all her grandchildren. She spotted him at the same time he did her, and walked toward him with her arms already outstretched. She palmed his cheeks and looked straight into his eyes. No one had a warmer heart than her, but damn her hands were cold.

"You are so handsome," she said. "But you look a little

thin. Are you eating enough?"

Bryce took her hands and warmed them with his. "Hello, grandma. You look lovely as ever."

"Thank you." She looked around briefly. "Now where's this girl you won't admit you're smitten with?"

"She should be here any minute."

"When she arrives, you bring her right over to me for an introduction, you hear?"

"Got it."

"Good." She nodded to someone over his shoulder. "Duty calls. I'll see you later." With a quick peck on his cheek, she dashed away like a woman half her age.

"Hey, dude," Danny said, handing him one of the beers in his hand. "To the man of the hour." They clinked bottles.

"Thanks." He took a swig before turning his attention to Olivia. "Hi, Liv. Thanks for coming tonight."

"Of course. These are the moments friends don't miss, right?"

Danny put his arm around her shoulders. "And don't worry, we won't play up the fan thing too much."

"Yeah, how about you keep all fanning to yourselves please."

"Your grandmother told me I'm allowed one catcall," Danny said.

"You kissed her hand, didn't you?"

"Yep." Danny grinned.

A flash of color caught the corner of Bryce's eye and he turned his head. His heart stopped. Honor stood beside Sophie and Zane dressed in an elegant short-sleeved floor length blue dress covered in sequins. Her dark blond hair fell in soft waves past her shoulders. Her lips showed off a glossy sheen.

From across the room their eyes met.

The sound of voices died. The tables, chairs, wait staff,

guests, all ceased to exist. One singular thing—one beautiful human being—held his attention.

"My date's here," he said to Danny and Liv. "I'll be back." He put his beer down on an empty tray table and strode toward her.

The closer he got, the sexier her smile grew. Light from the hanging chandeliers seemed to catch each tiny bead on her gown and she shimmered more breathtaking than the ocean under a full moon.

"Hi," he said, kissing her cheek in greeting.

"Hi."

"You look incredible."

"Thank you. You do, too."

"Congratulations, bro," Zane said, patting him on the back and breaking his connection with Honor.

"Congratulations," Sophie echoed, wrapping him in a hug.

"Thanks. I need to steal this beautiful woman away for a few," Bryce said. "We'll catch up with you guys at the table." He tucked Honor's arm in his, and while he really wanted to whisk her away somewhere private, he searched out his grandmother instead.

"Where are we going?" she whispered.

"Worried?"

"Yes."

He paused. She'd gotten quiet last night at dinner and she seemed a little off now. He'd half expected her to cancel on him at the last minute. But here she was and he didn't want her worrying her bottom lip. Or pulling away from him.

"There's no reason to be nervous," he said, fighting the impulse to run the pad of his thumb over that full lip of hers. "You're my guest tonight. That's it."

The nonchalant words did the trick and eased the tension creasing her forehead. She nodded. *His* muscles, however, suddenly tensed. With the truth about Payton's list, they'd taken a big step forward. But it seemed two steps back always followed.

"But my grandmother did request a private introduction." He resumed walking toward the sound of a very distinct laugh.

Honor brought him to a stop. "Now? I just got here and that seems..." She pulled in a deep breath. "Really quick."

Bryce squeezed her arm. "She likes to know everyone at her table before she butters her bread, that's all." Truth. Mostly.

"So this isn't anything significant?"

"No," he lied.

"Oh. Okay." Honor gave a confident nod of her head. "Let's go meet her then. She sounds like my kind of grandma."

"She's everyone's kind," he said proudly, resuming their stride. "And there she is." With a few more steps they reached her.

"Grandma, this is Honor Mitchell. Honor, my grandmother, Ruth Bishop."

"Honor." She took Honor's hands in both of hers. "It's a pleasure to meet you."

"You, too."

"Your gown is resplendent." She held onto one of Honor's hands and lifted it up and out to the side.

"Thank you. I bought it in a small boutique. The owner designs and makes dresses and this is one of them. Your dress is also stunning."

His grandmother lowered their arms and gave a little wink. "We both like a little sparkle."

The smile Honor gave his grandmother did a number on his insides. "We do."

"And what is this?" Grandmother turned Honor's wrist over and narrowed her eyes at the tattoo. "Faith. I like that. Does it have special meaning?"

Honor's eyes flicked to his for a charged moment. "It

does. It was my best friend's middle name."

"Was?"

"Grandma."

"It's okay," Honor said. "She passed away almost a year ago."

Bryce put his hand on the small of Honor's back even though from the strength of her voice, she didn't need any comforting.

"I've been thinking about getting a tattoo myself," his grandma said, a twinkle in her eye. "One of those cute skull and bones, I think."

"Not the badass one?" Bryce teased, used to his grandmother's youthful vim and vigor.

"Don't tempt me, mister."

"Excuse me, Mrs. Bishop? A quick word before we begin?" said the woman Bryce thought was head of public relations for the foundation.

His grandmother smiled warmly at Honor. "Excuse me, would you? We'll talk more during dinner." She cast Bryce a quick look of affection—and approval—and took her leave.

"I like her," Honor said with tenderness.

"I'm pretty sure she loved you." He watched Honor's eyes widen just enough for him to know his use of the L word affected her. "So listen, I'd like another date with you after this."

She swallowed. He did, too. Her brother stood between them, knots of uncertainty deep in his gut, too, but he was powerless to stop himself from asking for more.

"I want to keep seeing you. I want to learn everything about you and have lots of amazing, sweaty sex." Damn, her blush turned him on. "I want to go places, do things, see the world through your eyes, too. What do you say?"

"I…" She took his face in her hands. "Okay."

His new favorite word. He grinned. From somewhere

over his shoulder, he heard his name being called. They broke apart, and he led her toward their table.

Danny, Zane, Liv, and Sophie were already sitting. His parents walked up at the same time as he and Honor. Bryce made introductions, his mom gushing over the Roseville pottery Honor had helped select. His father cornered him about work, asking questions Bryce didn't have all the answers to yet, but that felt strangely okay.

During dinner he and the guys talked sports while Honor and the girls talked other stuff. They ate, laughed, shared stories.

And whenever possible, Bryce held Honor's hand under the table.

• • •

Honor couldn't ever remember feeling so much a part of something. Sitting with Bryce and his family and friends—her friends too—a sense of belonging filled her. These people didn't know about her past, they knew her present, and their interest and kindness made her feel good. Made her feel like *she was good*.

As everyone finished their flourless chocolate cake, her stolen conversation with Sophie after dinner last night flitted through her mind.

"I'm so far from mastering who I am, Soph. How can I possibly be good to someone else?" Honor had said.

"You're good to everyone," Sophie answered.

"Not all the time. I eventually screw up."

"Why?"

"I don't know."

"Yes you do."

Silence, then Honor said, "How do you know?"

"How do I know you know or how do you know?"

"This is one of those moments where you've gone way over my head, Ms. Smarty Pants."

"I know you know because we can all answer the question, why? It's just a matter of being honest with yourself."

"Bryce deserves someone who doesn't have to ask why."

"You should let Bryce decide what he deserves. I personally think it's you."

"I'm terrified that I'll hurt him."

"So don't."

"He wants babies."

"He told you that?

"Did you see him tonight?"

"You don't want kids one day?"

"I don't know," Honor said frustrated. "I don't know anything right now."

"Mr. Bryce Bishop," said a disembodied voice over a microphone. Honor let her recollection go.

Bryce gave her hand a squeeze and flashed that amazing smile of his before standing. Applause filled the ballroom.

He stood at the podium so handsome and confident. Sincerity sounded in his every word. Compassion. Gratitude. Honor couldn't take her eyes off him. All night he'd been carefully attentive with subtle touches and whispers in her ear. He'd included her in conversations, asked her opinion on things, praised her.

His gaze landed on hers once again, and she imagined starting every day looking into those gorgeous dark pools.

*I love you.*

No, no, no.

Yes, yes, yes.

She did. She loved him.

In all honesty, she'd loved him the second she'd laid eyes on him. But getting stuck in a closet with him had sealed her ultimate fate. She blamed his kiss. One touch of his lips on hers and he'd cast a spell she couldn't break.

He ended his speech and returned to the table. Pride overflowed inside her like a living, breathing thing. She couldn't help but lean over and kiss his cheek, which freaked her out. Because his family and friends watched them.

Sophie touched her arm. "I'm not feeling very well so Zane and I are going to head out. I'm assuming Bryce will bring you home?"

All of a sudden the weight of Honor's realization brought her blood flow to a crashing halt. Her palms got sweaty, her face burned. Her breath came at an abnormally rapid rate. She needed air and time to think.

"Actually, I'm not feeling that great either. Would you mind if I caught a ride with you guys?"

"Of course not."

"Hey," Bryce said softly. "Everything okay?"

She turned to face him. "Yes, but I'm feeling a little out of sorts so I'm going to head home with Sophie and Zane."

"I'll take you."

"No." She put her hand on his thigh. "You should stay."

Disappointment marred his handsome features and she felt horrible for lying. But if she didn't hurry and leave there was a good chance she'd blurt out her affection for him and she didn't want to do that.

She wasn't sure she'd ever have the courage to do it.

• • •

Bryce watched Honor walk away with Zane and Sophie and his heart hurtled to the back of his throat. She had made his evening better. She made every minute of every day better. And even though he wasn't sure he could trust her not to break his heart, he didn't care.

She'd kissed him in front of everyone. That had to mean

something.

So she'd run.

He understood her fear. Hell, he felt it, too. His self control took a nosedive when he stood anywhere near her.

His parents and grandmother wrapped him in compliments and said their good-byes. "She's a keeper," his grandma whispered in his ear. The Bishop matriarch held the best judge of character of anyone he knew and he murmured back, "Thanks."

Not "I think so, too," because he didn't want to get his grandma's hopes up. Or his own.

"Bar," Danny said. "We're not through with you."

"Now," Olivia said, hooking his arm.

The two of them had always teamed up. He could say no, but they wouldn't listen.

They sat at a tall, round cocktail table in the dimly lit bar. A waitress stopped to take their order. "Three vodka tonics," Danny said.

"You got it, sugar." Her southern drawl drew a smile from his friend. Danny was a sucker for a girl with an accent.

"Damn." Danny watched her walk away.

Olivia rolled her eyes. And that's all it took to get the competition on. They'd played the accent game countless times before, and Bryce was grateful for the distraction. Danny started with his best attempt at an Irish brogue. It sounded like he needed to be put out of his misery. Liv laughed so hard she had tears in her eyes. She nailed a Bronx accent next. Bryce did his Crocodile Dundee. They kept at it until a guy sitting at the next table ambled over and declared Liv the winner. He also asked for her phone number. Danny told him to get lost. Serious American accent.

An hour later they were home. Liv took Danny's room, Danny the couch. Bryce thrashed around in bed as sleep eluded him. He couldn't get Honor out of his head. He sat up and lifted his phone from the bedside table.

*Legend says when you can't sleep at night it's because you're awake in someone else's dream*, he texted to Honor. She probably wouldn't see it since it was well after midnight. But she'd wake in the morning and know he'd been thinking of her.

*Shame we're both awake then*, she texted right back.

He smiled at the phone. Something had shifted in her eyes tonight while he'd stood up on stage and he'd wondered if she'd changed her mind about them dating. If it was emotions she wanted to hide from, then fine. He'd stick to their physical connection. Anything to keep her close for as long as possible.

*A damn shame since I know exactly what I'd be doing to you in dreamland.*

*Oh? What's that?*

Bryce's pulse picked up. Other parts of him tightened as he pictured Honor naked in her bed. *How about you pretend your hands are my hands and I describe in detail what to do with them?*

*Only if you play too.*

He pushed the covers off his overheated body, more than ready to play. Two seconds later she answered her phone practically before it rang.

"Honor's Hidden Pleasures. How may I serve you?" His smile grew impossibly wide. Her soft sexy voice made him ache. Her playfulness relieved his worry about the two of them.

"Take off everything you have on," he instructed, his tone gruff.

"Yes, sir."

Bryce had no idea how much time passed, so absorbed in Honor and their dirty talk that it did feel like a dream. They were in perfect sync, hit the mark and came at the same time. Her gasps of pleasure kept him semi-hard.

"Best dream ever," she said in a soft, sexy voice.

If only they didn't have to wake up.

# Chapter Thirteen

The traffic on Tuesday afternoon sucked. He should have taken Wilshire instead of Santa Monica. Or better yet, a helicopter. After sitting bumper to bumper for almost an hour, Bryce wanted to tear the steering wheel out. Instead, he let his thoughts wander to the peace and quiet of White Strand Cove. And to a certain blonde. On his way to meet Cooper for lunch, dread and eagerness filled him. The kid had requested the meeting and Bryce hoped it was good news. But he didn't want to give up Honor. Could he have that conversation with her brother? Bryce wanted the win-win.

A horn blared as Bryce pressed on the brakes to avoid the car that suddenly veered into his lane. A motorcyclist almost took out his side view mirror. Catching the next left, he pulled into an underground parking structure. He'd walk a couple of extra blocks.

His heart skidded to a stop when he got to the burger joint and found Cooper *and Honor* sitting at a table waiting for him. What was she doing here?

"Sorry, I'm late," he said, taking the seat next to Honor

and across from Cooper. "Hi, Honor. I didn't know you'd be joining us." He tried to gauge her reaction to his appearance, but she remained neutral.

Cooper didn't know about them.

"It was a last minute thing. I hope you don't mind," she said.

"Honor helped me figure some stuff out and I wanted her to be here. She's not happy about me going pro, so I thought she might feel better hearing us talk." Cooper lifted his glass and took a sip of what looked like lemonade.

Bryce forced himself to keep his eyes on Cooper and not his beautiful sister. "I take it you've made a decision about representation?" Jake Harrington had been bad mouthing Bryce and Danny all week. Bryce had no idea if Coop believed trash talk like that, but he was prepared to defend himself if need be.

"I want you to be my agent."

Relief and an insane amount of happiness filled Bryce's chest. "Fantastic." He extended his arm across the table to shake Coop's hand. "Welcome to Bishop-Ellis. We're really excited to have you."

"Thanks. I'm happy to join your team. I think you're the kind of person I need on my side."

Bryce put his forearms on the table. "What kind of person is that?"

"The kind of agent who doesn't put dollar signs before a client's health and safety."

The waitress stopped at their table and asked what they'd like to eat. While placing their orders his knee bumped Honor's. The innocent touch scorched like a silent command he stake his claim on Honor now. They exchanged glances. His body ached to get closer, to cover hers skin to skin.

"That's a pretty big deal to my family," Coop continued, drawing Bryce's attention away from Honor. *Stay focused, dude.* "Honor and I talked on Sunday and she mentioned you'd been in a serious accident when you were younger."

The familiar lump that always lodged in Bryce's throat when he thought about his accident prevented him from speaking. He nodded.

Honor's hand squeezed his thigh. The gentle pressure excited and soothed him at the same time. His eyes cut to hers for a brief moment.

"You know what it feels like to fight back to being whole again. A lot of people still look at me with sympathy and I hate that. Like I'm not ever gonna be the same as I was. Did that happen to you?"

"It did. Even my doctors thought I'd always walk with a limp."

Coop smiled. "You showed them."

"Yup."

"Zane also told me I'd be an idiot to go with anyone but you. He said you weren't the most cutthroat, but you were the most dedicated."

Bryce settled back in his chair. "I agree with that."

"So what happens next?" Coop asked.

"I'll have Danny write up the contract and we'll get a copy to you to sign. If you've got concerns let me know and we can talk about them."

"Cool."

"You'll keep him safe," Honor said. Question? Statement? It was hard to tell which one.

Bryce met those passionate, earnest blue eyes of hers again and he couldn't help himself. He reached across the table and took her hand. "I can't promise he'll never get hurt. Accidents happen. But I can promise to do everything in *my* power to keep him out of harm's way."

"Thank you." She rolled her lips together like they were parched and the urge to kiss her overwhelmed him.

Cooper cleared his throat, disapproval in his eyes. "Is there something going on with you two? I thought we understood each other where my sister's concerned."

"What?" Honor said.

"We did, but—"

"What are you guys talking about?" Honor interrupted before Bryce could come clean to Cooper.

"I told Bryce you were off limits. My career and my family don't mix."

Honor looked back and forth between him and Cooper. "You can't butt into my life like that, Coop. Who I see is none of your business."

"It is if it affects me."

"How would my seeing Bryce affect you?"

Cooper canted his head down as if to say *really*? "I love you H, but you've got like a two date rule. It would be really uncomfortable for me when things didn't work out with you two because I'd have to take your side. And that would suck for my partnership with him."

"I can keep my personal and professional life separate," Bryce said. "As far as I'm concerned, whatever happens between your sister and I has no bearing on what happens between us. As my client, you've got me 100 percent."

"I appreciate that," Cooper said. He put his arms on the table. "But I can't separate things so easily. And if you broke my sister's heart, I'd have to find a new agent."

Bryce let that sink in. He got it. He thought about his sister and imagined her dating one of his clients. Cooper even. If the relationship ended, Bryce would be in a tough spot. He'd defend and honor his sister until his last breath, and he'd be in the uncomfortable position of having to remain professional with the douche that caused her pain.

The unsettling truth set in. He couldn't have Cooper and Honor.

"Why didn't you tell me you and Coop had talked about this?" Honor asked, her irritated tone breaking into his thoughts.

"Things are that serious?" Cooper said.

Shit.

Think, Bishop, think. Right here, right now, what was he willing to risk? What did he want?

The answer came quickly and easily.

"Could I have a few minutes alone with your sister?" he said to Coop.

Cooper looked at Honor. She nodded. "Okay, I'll just eat my burger over at the bar," he said, taking the plate out of the waitress's arms as he stood. Bryce and Honor were served their meals.

A few seconds ticked by, both of them still, the wild beat of Bryce's heart pounding in his ears. He'd known the truth for a while now, but had been too chicken to acknowledge it. Not until he'd been forced to make a decision.

"I can't do this," Honor blurted out.

"What?" He hadn't heard her right.

"Whatever we've been doing, it's over."

Bryce's clothes felt two sizes too small. His throat burned hotter than the Mojave Desert. "It's not over."

"It is."

"Because of Cooper? Because of how he feels?" He took her hand. She pulled it away.

"No. Not because of Coop." Her words came out in a rush, her breathing uneven. "Or not just because of him. I'm not the right girl for you, Bryce."

"What are you talking about? You're—"

"Don't say perfect. Please don't say anything. I can't deal with all these feelings. I'm not capable of handling them without hurting you." She blinked, her eyes darted to the table, the floor, his chest, her lap, everywhere but at his face.

"What happened with Lance, it would destroy me if I caused someone pain like that again."

"Honor." It killed him to see her so upset. She was capable. If she'd just believe in herself like he did.

"I'm not a white picket fence kind of girl. You want babies and commitment." She let out another shaky breath.

His chest squeezed. He did want those things. And he knew she didn't. Had he been fooling himself into believing their casual affair meant as much to her as it did to him? That he could change her?

"And someone who will follow through on her promises."

"You follow—"

"Maybe. Eventually. But right now I can only concentrate on one thing. And that one thing should be me."

He stared at her profile. She wouldn't even look him in the eye when she blew him off. The one thing he hadn't pegged her for was selfish, which proved he didn't know her at all.

"I wish you could see yourself through my eyes," he said. Despite the beating she flung at him, his heart still wanted her.

She tossed her napkin onto her untouched meal and stood. "Cooper deserves you more than I ever could. I hope this doesn't mean he's lost you." Her eyes met his and he nearly broke seeing her unshed tears. "Let him know I'm waiting outside while you two finish up."

Bryce forced himself to stay in his chair, rather than run after her. He watched her walk away because that's what *she* wanted.

• • •

Honor turned on the shower. While the water heated she brushed her teeth, her attention on the sink bowl. She knew what she'd find if she looked in the mirror—the same sad

Sandy face that had stared back at her all week. She hated that face.

Her nose twitched as she wiped her mouth on a towel. Steam billowed around the ceiling and she closed her eyes as she shut the shower door and stood under the warm spray of—

"What the!" She stepped to the side and studied the water spilling from the showerhead. The smell she'd gotten a faint whiff of intensified. Was that chicken soup?

She stomped out of the shower, wrapped a towel around herself and threw open the bathroom door.

"April Fools!" Coop shouted.

"What in the world did you do?"

"I put a chicken bouillon cube inside the shower head so you could—"he laughed"—marinate."

Honor watched him crack himself up. "I hate you." But to be fair, she pretty much hated everything nowadays.

He stopped laughing and pulled a small gift box from behind his back. "No you don't. Happy birthday."

She snagged the gift. "Thank you. Now you take this shower and I'll take the next one."

"Open it," he said blocking the hallway so she couldn't get by.

"You're wasting water."

"I'm not getting in there until the cube has dissolved. Give it a few minutes. Now open." He nodded to the gift.

"Nice wrap job." She tore off the pretty paper and opened a plain white box.

"I had some help," he said shamelessly.

Tears pricked the back of her eyes when she saw business cards inside. She pulled one out and stared at the perfect font and perfect amount of information regarding Driftwood.

"Thank you." She wrapped her arms around his shoulders.

"Whoa." He stepped back. "Put some clothes on first."

"If only someone hadn't ruined my shower." She bopped him on the head.

He brushed off his sleeve with a boyish simper that would have been annoying had the prank not been pretty brilliant. "Had to keep the tradition alive."

Since he was five years old he'd played tricks on her. Some worked. Some didn't. It annoyed her growing up, but her mom would always say, "He plays jokes on you because he loves you and wants your attention."

Emotion clogged the back of the throat. Today was probably the last prank he'd pull on her. He'd decided to move to LA and live with a couple of other professional skateboarders. His career was about to kick into high gear and she couldn't be happier for him.

"You all right?" he asked.

She nodded. What else was she going to do? Tell him she missed Bryce so much it physically hurt to think about him?

No. Ending their relationship *was* for the best. Just because she loved Bryce didn't mean she deserved a happily ever after. She eventually failed people. This time she'd been saved from inflicting harm as well. She'd done Bryce a favor.

"You're full of shit," Coop said.

"*What?*" Who said he could call her out? And on her birthday.

"There's something bothering you," Coop said quietly. "And you don't usually shut me out."

The tall, skinny kid in front of her was way too smart. And so damn sincere she wanted to cry. She did normally tell him things, but she couldn't this time. What was best for her brother was Bryce and she'd gladly suffer so *they* had a strong relationship.

"It's nothing. I think I'm just missing mom and dad. Plus, I'm worried about opening Driftwood and being behind on things for the Spring Fair."

He squinted like he didn't totally buy it. "I can help with whatever you need."

She wished that were true. "I know."

"I've got to head out, but I'll be home by six to go to dinner. And I'm getting you drunk if your attitude hasn't changed."

"We'll see," she said to his retreating back. "Wait, what about a shower?"

"I already took one," he sang out. Jerk.

She took a cold, but clean shower, dressed in one of her favorite T-shirt dresses, made her bed, folded clothes that didn't need to be folded, cleaned up the mess on her nightstand, blow dried her hair, made Coop's bed, and picked his dirty clothes up off the floor and threw them in his hamper. Basically, she did everything she could to keep her mind occupied until Sophie arrived.

Someone pounded on her door. She hurried to answer it.

"Your doorbell squirted me in the face," Sophie said, wiping at her eye.

"I'm going to kill my brother. Sorry about that." Honor pulled the gag doorbell off the door. "Coop gets a little carried away on April Fool's day."

Sophie grinned as she eyed the real doorbell off to the side. "I don't think I've ever been pranked before. That was a good one."

"We'll plot our revenge on our way. Let's go." Honor shut the door behind her. "You look good today."

"Thanks. I told myself it was mind over matter. No way was I letting this little one interfere with our plans." Sophie absently rubbed her stomach before putting an arm around Honor. "Happy birthday!"

They arrived at Pretty in Pink a few minutes later. Being inside the nail salon was like walking into a decked out cotton candy cloud with crystal chandeliers. "The birthday girl is here!" Maggie announced.

"Hi, Mags." Honor hugged her friend and shop owner.

"Hi, Maggie," Sophie said.

Maggie gave Sophie a wide smile and wrapped her in a gentle hug. "How is our mommy-to-be?"

"She's great."

"Good. Let's get you guys started." Maggie put them next to each other in spa chairs for the full mani/pedi treatment.

Conversation flowed and for the first time in days, Honor's thoughts quieted. When Maggie brought out a birthday cake with candles and had everyone in the salon sing, Honor put on a happy face for real.

The shop quieted down and two twenty-something girls walked in. They sat across the room from her and Sophie. Honor didn't recognize them and they kept talking to each other with barely a glance to anyone else.

"So, yeah, she really messed him up," the shorter of the girls said.

"Sounds like. What kind of person does that to a guy?" the taller girl said.

Short Girl shrugged. "A selfish one, I guess? He knows I love him, but I'm afraid after what he's been through, he'll never fully commit. I'm wondering if I should break things off."

Tall girl put a hand on her friend's arm. "I'm sorry, Hannah, but maybe give Lance a little more time?"

Honor's breath caught. Her foot slipped off its perch and made a splash in the tub of warm water. Lance had left for college in San Diego and stayed there after graduation. Honor had heard he was seeing someone. Someone named Hannah.

"Maybe," Hannah said. Her gaze connected with Honor's and for a split second Honor wondered if Hannah knew she was the selfish girl who had messed Lance up.

The room shrank and Honor had to concentrate to keep

her disposition even.

"Honor?"

She turned her head to Maggie. "Looks yummy. Thanks." She took the piece of offered cake and dug in. With each bite her head swam.

She'd thought she'd turned the corner on her past, but here it was, dragging her back down.

# Chapter Fourteen

The next morning Honor put on her running shoes and hit the beach. The early morning surf rolled gently onto shore, clouds hid the sun. She started off slowly, leaving deep footprints in the hard, wet sand. A few surfers floated in the mellow tide. A guy waved a metal detector back and forth. In the distance she saw another jogger heading toward her.

For a moment she almost dropped to her knees, fatigue and lack of sleep telling her body to stop moving. But that wouldn't do. Stopping meant her heart would have nothing else to do but ache.

She'd woken at the crack of dawn with a killer hangover and one thought: It *was* time to concentrate on herself and ditch the pain eating her up inside. And the best start? A run. A run until her lungs burned and her heart pounded and the suffocating feeling of loss and loneliness was sweated out of her. She picked up her pace.

If she worked her muscles until they protested, revved her pulse as high as it could go, and let the wind rushing past her take her stupid thoughts with it, then she could start fresh.

Rediscover the Honor Payton had hoped she would.

And, she would.

Forget a juice cleanse. This was going to work way faster. It had to.

Not that she had any delusions of falling out of love with Bryce in the next hour. Which really sucked. There should be a love switch. Or a clapper! Clap on—I love you. Clap off—Not anymore!

But maybe she could forgive herself for her mistakes.

She pumped her arms faster and concentrated on her stride. The beach stretched for miles. She could—would—make this happen. Her sanity obviously depended on it. Who in their twenties knew what the heck a clapper was?

She increased her pace. Her feet slapped the sand. She wiped her forehead, the first beads of sweat finally wetting her skin. With every deliberate stride, she blanked her mind and focused on the shoreline. Nothing else.

"Honor?"

Her gaze flew to the jogger about to pass her by. She stopped. He stopped. A weight plunged from the back of her throat to the pit of her stomach.

"Lance?"

"Yeah."

They looked awkwardly at one another as if they had no idea how to act. "Hi," she finally said, catching her breath with her hands on her thighs.

"It's good to see you," Lance said.

"It is?" she asked surprised.

He palmed the back of his neck. "I was actually hoping I'd run into you while I was here. I wanted to apologize," he said.

"*What*?" she squeaked out, lifting her torso.

"I said some pretty awful things to you the last time we saw each other and …" His gaze dropped to the sand. He toed the granules with his shoe.

"I deserved what you said," she whispered.

He looked up, his kind blue eyes just like she remembered them. "No, you didn't. I was hurt, yeah. But I wasn't an idiot. I knew I was pushing you for something you weren't ready for. What I did?" He took a deep breath. "I did to hurt you more than myself."

She shivered, from the cool breeze or his admission, she didn't know for sure. "What do you mean?"

"I wanted to punish you. I wanted everyone to hate you. That night at prom, all the guys teased me and wouldn't let up on the jokes. I snapped."

"Lance—"

"I was the guy who had it all. My first choice college, the cool car, the best girlfriend. What I wasn't, was as mature as I thought I was. The stunt I pulled proved that."

"I still hurt you. Messed you up."

"You didn't mess me up. That was my college girlfriend. She cheated on me."

*Wait. What?*

"I was pissed at you, Honor. Even hated you for a while. But what happened is on me, not you, and I wanted to say I'm sorry."

Honor's balance wobbled. "I'm sorry, too."

"I know. You told me that day, but I didn't want to hear it." He took a breath. "I, uh, proposed to my girlfriend last night. She said yes. She's amazing and she loves me. Faults and all."

"That's…" Goosebumps broke out on Honor's arms. "That's great. Congratulations. I'm really happy for you."

"Thanks."

"Does she know what happened with us?"

"No. Not yet. I didn't want to keep drudging up the past. So, anyway, I'm glad we ran into each other."

Honor chuckled. "Ran being the operative word."

He smiled. "Yeah. Take care of yourself."

"I will. You, too." She smiled back, nothing big, but more genuine than she'd felt in the last week.

She resumed her run, but a funny thing happened as she picked up her pace. She felt light on her feet, like the weight of her biggest mistake had finally been lifted from her shoulders.

It had.

Her breath hitched. Perfect didn't exist, not even close, but forgiving herself once and for all, was a big step toward a better tomorrow. She made a sharp right and ran up the beach toward the boardwalk. Cut through an alleyway, headed up Ocean, and landed on Main Street. The smell of coffee and cinnamon wafting through the air like vapor from a genie's bottle tried to lure her toward the Beach Café.

She fought the temptation, telling herself she risked running into the Street Team if she didn't hightail it. Those pesky ladies hadn't let up one bit this past week, asking where Bryce was and commenting on how "hunky" they found him and what a great catch.

He was that and more. And even if it was too late, it was time she told him how she really felt.

• • •

Bryce sat at his desk getting absolutely nothing done. He could not wrap his head around a damn thing. Correction. He had laser sharp focus when it came to Honor and driving himself crazy with memories of her laugh, the softness of her skin, the texture of her hair. Her kiss.

He'd set out to shed his good guy image. Have some fun without getting serious. Save his heart from another break. Idiot.

Pressing a hand to his temple to stop the throbbing,

he wished like hell he wasn't still so conscious of her smell, her taste, the way her eyes smiled before her lips followed. The way she walked and the sweet, sexy sound of her voice. Without being near, she surrounded him.

He… he loved her.

Despite her fear of love and commitment, he'd fallen completely in love and never should have let her walk away. That was on him and he hated himself for it.

She challenged him. Made his life worthwhile. She'd saved him from believing he didn't have a heart left to give. He ran his hand across his chest. She owned his heart and it was time to fight to win hers.

"Cooper's here," Danny said, walking through the door of Bryce's office with Coop trailing behind him.

"Hey, Cooper," Bryce said. "Thanks for coming in on such short notice."

Danny took one of the two chairs on the other side of Bryce's desk and motioned for Coop to take the other. Once seated, his newest client looked around the room before saying, "No problem. If this is about the contract, my dad said he had one minor change and you should have it in your email later today."

"Great. Thanks. But I asked you here to talk about your sister."

Danny glanced at him, then Coop, then back to Bryce again. "What's going on?"

"I was about to ask the same thing," Coop said.

Bryce looked straight at Cooper. "I wasn't exactly honest with you about Honor. The truth is I'm in love with your sister and if that means you sign with another agent, then that's the way it goes. Because I can't let *her* go.

Coop scratched the side of his head.

Danny raised his eyebrows.

"It's been a hell of a week and I haven't stopped thinking

about her. She's the one for me. I'll never do anything to hurt her so if you decide to stay with me, you'll never have to pick sides."

"That's it," Cooper said with dawning recollection.

Bryce leaned his arms on his desk. "What's it?"

"Why she's been a total sad case this past week and wouldn't tell me why. It's you. But the past couple months make sense now, too. It was like she'd swallowed a happy pill and I think you're the reason. She's been broken for a really long time and you fixed her." He brushed at the corner of his eye, and Bryce kind of fell in love with the kid.

"I'm not sure I deserve—"

"I think you do. So even though I'm still worried about my sister and my agent being together, I don't want to be the reason she doesn't get a chance with you."

Bryce wanted nothing less than to give Honor everything. "I appreciate that."

"And I don't want to give you up either."

"I'm happy to hear you say that, too. I've got big plans for you."

Cooper smiled. "Awesome."

"It sounds like I've got a good chance of making things right with your sister, but you in if I need some help?"

"For sure. But don't worry. Everything's gonna work out." He stood and put out his hand. Bryce did the same and they shook. "As far as any details about you and my sister, though. You can keep those to yourself."

Bryce chuckled. "I'll let Honor keep you posted."

"Cool. See you guys." He lifted his chin in good-bye to Danny and Bryce sat back down.

Danny put his hands behind his head. "Well, well, well. So that's been the reason for that sad bonehead face of yours."

"How do you know it's not because of you?"

"You're not getting rid of me altogether, dude." His best

friend had finally shared what had been on his mind—he wanted out of the agent world so he could focus on what he really loved: woodworking. Over the past couple of weeks they'd worked to make that happen. Hired someone new. They'd always be friends, just not partners.

"You know I'm not surprised," Danny said with a smug look on his face.

"I know."

"Are you sure Honor will still want you?"

"Have I told you what a pain in the ass you are?"

"Numerous times."

"You really need to get your own love life so you stay out of mine."

"You've no idea." Danny's shoulders slumped.

Bryce narrowed his eyes at his friend. "Is there something you're not telling me?"

Danny quickly masked whatever it was Bryce had seen. "You heading to White Strand?"

"The thought crossed my mind." Honor might have technically walked out on him, but he'd been the one to let her go without telling her what she meant to him first.

"Go big or go home."

Bryce scratched under his chin. How many times had he said that? How many times had he heard it? "Thanks for the reminder."

"Don't mention it." Danny stood. "Any other problems I can solve for you this afternoon?"

"I'm good."

Danny gave a salute and left. Bryce laced his fingers behind his head and stared at the signed hockey stick leaning against the corner of the wall. His gaze shifted to other signed memorabilia on the bookshelf.

On his desk sat a framed note from his sister. She'd given it to him after his bike accident. Used colored pencils to spell out his name vertically, then attached a nice word to each letter.

Words alone didn't always go the distance. But words combined with action could do some serious damage. And he needed to do something serious to convince Honor to give them a chance. He jumped to his feet.

"I need your help," he said, barging into Danny's office. Bryce staggered for a second, seeing boxes packed up.

"You okay?" Danny stood from behind his nearly bare desk.

"Yeah." He let out the breath he'd been holding since the day Danny told him about his new plans. "I'm just going to miss you around here."

Danny grinned. "Aww."

"Shut up."

"So, what kind of help?" Danny eased back into his chair.

Bryce launched into what he envisioned, watching Danny nod in agreement. They made a plan and on his way out of the office Bryce called Zane and Sophie. To make this work, he needed them, too.

And a small town named White Strand Cove.

• • •

"Could you slow it down to a human pace, please?" Honor said, trying to keep up with her brother. When she'd agreed to go grab coffee and a fritter with him she hadn't realized she'd signed up for a speed walk, too.

"You really need to get back to exercising," Coop said, not slowing down in the least.

"I'll have you know I went running last weekend."

"Really?"

"And I walk *all* the time. But jeez, what's the rush this morning?" The sun shone, birds sang, flowers bloomed. Spring had sprung and she wanted to enjoy it.

Those seemed to be the magic words because he lagged enough for her to join his side. "Sorry. I'm just hungry," he said.

She bumped his elbow with hers. "You're always hungry."

They turned the corner onto Main and Honor sighed as the smell of baked goodness and coffee hit her nose. "Where is everyone this morning?" she asked, not really expecting Coop to give her an answer. It was just awfully quiet for a Friday morning. Usually the line for fritters busted out the door.

Weirder still, when they pushed open the door to the Beach Café not a single person stood inside. That had *never* happened in Honor's entire existence. If Rachel hadn't smiled from behind the counter, Honor would've thought she'd entered some alternate universe.

"Morning!" Rachel said, a little too perky.

Then Coop ran back outside like someone had yelled "fire." What the heck was going on? The way the hair on the back of her neck stood up, she was about to get punked or enter the Twilight Zone.

What she didn't expect was to hear Bryce's voice from somewhere behind the counter. In the kitchen maybe?

Her pulse hammered. She'd thought to reach out to him this weekend and here he was, like her wish had been granted.

"Have a seat," Rachel said. "There." She nodded to Honor's right.

That's when Honor noticed a computer sat on one of the round tables. She walked over and took the chair in front of it.

"Don't move," Rachel said before disappearing into the back.

Not a problem, since she'd decided to stay glued to her seat until someone told her what to do. Because all of a sudden it seemed vitally important she not make one wrong move.

Bryce.

Was here.

Why?

"There's a song from the Beatles," he said, coming out from behind the register.

Honor blinked several times and swallowed. She'd dreamed about seeing him over and over again, but coming face to face with him for real was a gazillion times better.

"The first verse is, 'Say the word and you'll be free.'"

She didn't know the song and still goose bumps popped up on her arms. Their eyes met and she gave silent thanks she had a chair underneath her because the sight of him made her weak in the knees. His hair was neat and tidy and she wanted to mess it up with her fingers. His blue button down shirt—the exact same color he'd worn the first night they'd met—was pressed and she wanted to wrinkle it. The top buttons were open and her pulse raced at the peek of smooth skin. But what really accelerated her heart was a glimpse of ink on his chest. Over his heart maybe? That killed her almost as much as the sexy cleft in his chin.

"Hi," he said, standing on the other side of the table, behind the computer.

"Hi," she said back.

"There's a second and third verse and then the fourth verse goes, 'Have you heard the word is love?'"

The love she had inside her for Bryce, it hadn't stopped. It wouldn't leave. She'd tried. And failed.

"Today I'm here to tell you, and show you, how much I love you, Honor Mitchell." He flashed that sexy smile of his, his eyes twinkled with admiration and affection, and she gripped the edge of her chair to keep from sliding off. He loved her!

"I love your hallux."

She burst out a laugh. He couldn't have started with a better word or better reminder of how much they just clicked.

He loved her big toe.

"Press enter on the keyboard, Honor."

Blinking back tears of joy, she did as he asked. The dark screen blinked to life and revealed a frozen image of the park in Town Square with... she looked a little closer... people holding some type of block.

"Hit play," he said.

Her breath caught as she watched Sophie, Zane, Coop, Danny, Jules and Dylan line up side-by-side on the monitor. They each held a large pale wooden block with a black letter painted on the front to spell out the word hallux. The blocks looked like Scrabble pieces with small numbers in the bottom right corner denoting point value.

"I love your smile," Bryce said next.

Sophie and the hallux gang put their blocks down on the grass and dispersed just as Midge and the Street Team, along with Mr. Case, hurried onto the screen with letters in their hands to spell out s-m-i-l-e.

"I love that you care more about others than you do yourself."

Honor continued to watch the video in awe as an overhead camera angle showed Midge's group put the letters down on the ground vertically, using the second "l" in hallux. Mr. Case took his "l" and hurried away as the mayor and his wife and others she'd known her whole life spelled out s-e-l-f-l-e-s-s.

Oh my god. Bryce was playing Scrabble, right there in the middle of town to show her what he loved about her. Tears pricked the back of her eyes again. Her whole body shook.

"I love your mind and your spirit and your laugh."

Using the "s" in smile, the blocks spelling selfless were laid on the ground just as a new group showed her l-a-u-g-h.

Honor covered her mouth with her hand. Some major

filmmaking, not to mention coordination had taken place to bring her this piece of magic.

"And I really love the way you osculate."

"In English please!" someone shouted on screen and she marveled that Bryce had timed his speech so perfectly with the video. He must have practiced.

"Kiss," Honor muttered, her eyes lifting to lock on Bryce's. She wanted to kiss his whole face. Hide the two of them away in her house and kiss him until next week.

The osculate group put their letters down and then the video cut to an overhead shot again. Honor stared at the screen, the words on the grass linking to form the most beautiful Scrabble puzzle she'd ever seen. Her heart leaped into her throat.

"I love *you*," Bryce said.

She looked back up to find he held his own block letter—U. His eyes sparkled with mischief and passion as he stepped around the table and took her hand to lead her outside. Then he slid the lid off the block and a bunch of colorful butterflies fluttered free. Her mouth fell open, she sighed in more happiness than she thought possible.

"Let me love you, Honor. Fly with me for the rest of our lives." He put the block down and took her in his arms. She could barely breathe, so overwhelmed by what he'd done.

"I love you," he repeated. "I know you're scared, but you're it for me. The love of my life."

"What about Cooper?" she asked.

"Cooper is fine with it!" Her brother shouted from a few yards away. In fact, the entire town had come out from hiding, huge grins on their faces. Uncle Tuck, Sophie, Dylan, the Street Team, Tango…

Bryce took her hand and rubbed his thumb across her knuckles. "I'm asking for a chance. Stay with me and we'll figure things out. No pressure." One side of his sexy mouth lifted. "At least not yet."

He wanted her and Lord knew she wanted him. "I do want to try. With you. Only you." Her life was better with him in it. So much better.

"Yeah?"

She cupped his cheek with her free hand. "I love you, too." She'd never said that to anyone before and feeling the euphoria inside her chest, she knew it was because she'd been waiting for him. "And was going to find you and tell you that this weekend."

"Well?" Uncle Tuck shouted. "What's the verdict?"

Bryce brought her closer and kissed her. Hard. Hoots and hollers rang out as his tongue pushed inside her mouth and he kissed her like they didn't have an audience. She didn't care. Too lost in the incredible sensation of having this man devour her and claim her as his.

"Thanks for coming to get me," she said breathlessly when they needed to come up for air. "I was secretly hoping somehow, some way, you would beat me to it."

"Always." He touched his forehead to hers.

He lifted away and family and friends zeroed in on them with hugs and pats on the back and words of praise for Bryce. Shirley told him he was better than the heroes in her romance novels.

Honor grabbed his hand and pulled him around the corner for some privacy. "I forgot to say thank you for that incredible video. It was amazing."

"You're amazing." He pushed her up against the side of the building and trapped her between his arms, his hands flat on the wall on either side of her head.

"I'll probably make a few mistakes." More like dozens, but he already knew that, right?

"Then I'll be there to catch you. And you'll be there to catch me."

"I will. Promise."

He lowered his head and kissed her neck, her collarbone. Her insides went all gooey. "Think anyone would notice if we got out of here?"

"Why Miss Mitchell, do you want me all to yourself?"

"Yes, I really do."

"Then what are we waiting for?"

# Chapter Fifteen

*Six weeks later...*

Honor stood at her dresser mirror to put on the yellow diamond earrings Bryce had just given her. "They're beautiful," she said, eyeing their sparkle.

He wrapped his arms around her waist and put his chin on her shoulder. "Because of the person wearing them." His hands slid down the sides of her legs and under her dress.

"Bryce," she said in warning.

"Yes?"

"We need to get going. I can't be late to my own opening." She'd done it. Finished all the preparations for Driftwood and tonight she'd invited everyone to help celebrate. Pride had been building steam inside her all day and she owed so much of that to Bryce. He'd helped her believe she could do it.

He pushed her in the right direction when she needed it, supported and listened to all her ideas, no matter how out there, and encouraged her to be the best version of herself. Her. Self. Not anyone else.

Following through on the business she and Payton had dreamed about meant more than words could say. More confident than ever, more committed than ever, her fears had all but disappeared. Tonight was only the beginning. And she knew without a doubt, Payton would be there with her in spirit. She twirled the infinity bracelets on her wrist.

"I'm thinking under five minutes, beautiful." He pressed his warm lips to her temple as his very skillful fingers marched up to her panties. Her skin sizzled. It took him all of three seconds to get her hot and bothered. If she were honest, she'd gotten turned on watching him dress. The way he buttoned a shirt? Zipped and buttoned his pants? It was like foreplay in reverse and she'd wanted to strip his clothes off him.

The tattoo over his heart didn't hurt either. *Honor*, it said.

"This is just mean." The best kind of mean. *Keep going.*

Their eyes met in the mirror. He cocked an eyebrow.

"You know I can't"—he grazed his thumb over her aroused center—"say no to you when you touch me like this."

"Want me to stop?" He dropped a kiss right by her earlobe.

"Don't you dare."

He smiled. "I do believe there's one spot left to christen." Really? She thought they'd christened the entire house since Coop moved out and Bryce moved in.

"Where's that?"

"Right here. Put your hands on the dresser, Ms. Mitchell." She did and he did the rest, sliding her panties down her legs, freeing himself from his dress pants, and lifting her dress to her waist. She heard the rustle of a condom and then he was at her opening. "Look in the mirror," he whispered.

His heated gaze met hers and with one smooth thrust he was inside her. Filling her. Loving her. He brushed her hair over one shoulder and rocked against her with a slow, steady pace. She gripped the edge of the dresser. They didn't once look away from each other. His hands roamed over her breasts, her stomach, the curls between her legs.

All his devastating kisses, his supportive words, the way he loved her body and her thoughts…She wasn't the same person she'd been a few months ago. He'd confessed he wasn't either, told her she was the something else to make his life worthwhile.

"You feel so damn good. But I promised to be quick," he murmured.

"Mmmm," was all she managed to get out. A whimper followed. With each stroke she grew more restless, her arousal more intense.

With his left hand he cupped her breast, rubbed his thumb over her nipple. With his right, he found the bundle of nerves just above where they were joined.

"I love you," he said.

Her body on fire from those three little words and his touch, she hit the point of no return and moaned his name as she came. He pressed his hips more firmly against her and followed right behind.

A sigh escaped him as he kissed her cheek. She turned her head and kissed him more fully. With one last taste of his lips, she pulled away. "Love you, too."

"It's time to go?" he asked. His tone suggested he wished they didn't have to, but she knew he was as excited about her store opening as she was.

She turned and tapped her nose to his. "Yes."

They righted themselves and hurried out the door. On the short drive into town he held her hand and told her how proud he was of her. She hoped by the time they got to the store, no one would notice her blush. Bryce's words from a few days ago flitted through her mind for the hundredth time.

*I don't want or need a fence. I want to live free*, he'd told her. *With you.*

*For always.*

She'd finally found where she belonged.

*With him.*

# Acknowledgments

Thank you to my amazing husband for supporting me, encouraging me, and always making me feel like I matter more than anything else. I love you.

Thank you to my awesome editors Wendy Chen and Stacy Abrams. You guys are the best and I am so grateful to you for your tireless input and guidance. Especially when it comes to help with the "C" word. <wink> Wendy, you're also the rock on which I rely, and from the bottom of my heart, thank you for your always kind words, support, and friendship.

Thank you to Debbie Suzuki, Tara Quigley, Alycia Tornetta, Jessica Cantor, and the entire Entangled team. You guys are fantastic and I'm so lucky to have you.

Thank you to Roxanne Snopek, for her tattoo expertise. Thank you to Cole McCade and all my FB friends who suggested a name for Honor and Payton's antique store. Thanks to everyone who chimed in and offered fun phrases. I can't get sha-to-the-zam out of my head!

And last, but not least, thank you to my readers. This is my tenth book. Ten! Which is crazypants. And all kinds of crazy good. And it wouldn't mean nearly as much as it does without you guys. Thank you so much for reading my books.

# About the Author

When not attached to her laptop, USA Today Bestselling Author Robin Bielman can almost always be found with her nose in a book. A California girl, the beach is her favorite place for fun and inspiration. Her fondness for swoon-worthy heroes who flirt and stumble upon the girl they can't live without jumpstarts all of her story ideas. She is a 2014 RITA Finalist, loves to frequent coffee shops, and plays a mean game of sock tug of war with her crazy-cute dog, Harry. She cherishes her family and friends and loves to connect with readers. Get the scoop on Robin, her books, and sign up for her newsletter on her website at http://robinbielman.com

*Discover the* **Kisses in the Sand** *series...*

## KEEPING MR. RIGHT NOW

Brainy, organized Sophie Birch is no beach bunny, but when a surf lesson introduces her to Zane Hollander, suddenly she's up close and personal with the world's sexiest surf star. But what can a great-looking, experienced athlete possibly see in a klutzy out-of-towner who's never set foot in the ocean? Zane sees Sophie as the perfect girl to help him reform his image and he can't resist her as she blooms under the beachy sun. But Zane knows he'll just break her heart, because nothing's more important to him than following the tide.

### *Also by Robin Bielman*

*Secret Wishes series*

## KISSING THE MAID OF HONOR

## HER ACCIDENTAL BOYFRIEND

## WILD ABOUT HER WINGMAN

*Take a Risk series*

## WORTH THE RISK

## RISKY SURRENDER

## HIS MILLION DOLLAR RISK

## YOURS AT MIDNIGHT

* 9 7 8 1 9 4 3 3 3 6 3 4 0 *